CORALEE TAYLOR

If I Were a Better Man

Fated Hearts of River View Book One

First edition

ISBN: 979-8-9914100-3-8

Cover art by Coralee Taylor
Illustration by Canva

This book was professionally typeset on Reedsy.
Find out more at reedsy.com

To all the recovering addicts, there is hope.
You are worthy of love and healing.
You deserve a seat at the table.
Keep Coming Back.
One Day At A Time.

Contents

Preface

If I Were A Better Man is book one in the Fated Hearts of River View series, written as a novella. It follows a mid-thirties MMC from a previous interconnected trilogy. To better understand the characters mentioned throughout the book, I suggest you read the Ties That Bind series, beginning with book one: **I See You, Charlotte**.

If you haven't read Charlotte's story but you plan to, don't go any further in this book. It will spoil the "who will she choose" theme throughout her trilogy.

Content/Trigger Warning

This book contains scenes that may be triggering. Please refer to the content warnings below. This list may not be all-inclusive. Your mental health and safety are important. If you feel that any of the below items would harm you in any way, this is not the book for you. Read on safely, my friends.

Triggers may include:
    Drug/Alcohol Use and Recovery
    SA/SV and Non-con (mentioned, not descriptive)
    Abuse
    Death
    Hospitalization
    Illness

Prologue

2004

"What's got you crying, darlin'?" I ask as she continues sobbing. Watching her fall apart in front of me while I can't do a damn thing about it is tearing my fucking heart out. I kneel before her. Her tiny body is jolting violently with the force of her tears. They are ripping her apart.

"Shh. Look at me. Can you do that for me, baby?"

She finally gazes up and fixes me with bloodshot eyes. I know whatever she's about to say is going to tear our world into something unrecognizable. We stare at each other for so long, mirroring our breaths and soaking in this moment. The moment before everything changes. The moment before she breaks my fucking heart.

"I'm leaving. Daddy's taking me to Tennessee." She laments in between hiccups and stuttered breaths.

"Y'all taking a trip, or...?" I ask although I reckon I don't really need to. If this was a temporary visit, she wouldn't be falling apart in front of me.

Her head shakes somberly, and the tears come again as she curls in on herself. I want to reach out and comfort her, fix her, shield her. But I remain frozen in place.

"No. Moving. Permanently."

Okay. Okay. We can deal with this. It may change our plans a bit, and we have another year of school left, but we can make this work. "Alright, we can make it work, sweetheart. Don't worry. We'll make it work." I tell her, full of conviction.

Her eyes soften as she peers back up at me, and my body fills with ice. She reaches a hand out and brushes an errant strand of my sandy blond hair off of my forehead. "I think it's best if we don't."

Crinkling my brow in confusion, I ask, "Don't what?"

"Make it work. I need a break. My family needs to heal, and I just don't think that's possible if we continue being together."

The sound of the rapidly galloping organ in my chest exploding into a thousand pieces should be deafening. The windows should be shattering. Car alarms beeping uncontrollably. But as I stare at my first love, the silence is suffocating. She's fucking leaving me.

As I continue staring through her, she stands and hugs me with all her little might. Her tears mark a path from her eyes down my cheek and find a home on my shirt collar. She presses her lips to my temple. I can feel the tremble through her kiss.

Before she pulls away and walks out on me for good, she whispers softly into my ear. "You will always be my first love, and I will *always* love you, Zachariah Thaddeus Morris."

I

Part One

God, grant me the serenity
to accept the things I cannot change,
courage to change the things I can,
and wisdom to know the difference.

Chapter 1

Step 1: Admitting powerlessness over addiction
Present Day

Sweat drips down my back as my body heaves violently over the toilet. The contents of my stomach have long since come and gone. Bile and maybe a fucking piece of lung are the only things leaving me at this point.

If I had known when I agreed to come to rehab that withdrawal would be this horrific, I might have chosen prison. At least there, I'd be able to get my hands on something to take the edge off.

My intestines contort like a coiling snake as more emptiness makes its way up my throat.

"Can you die any fucking louder, bro?" My roommate, Harrison, groans from his cozy position on his bed. I can't pull away to give him a tongue lashing, so I reach back and flip him off as another wave of nausea crashes, and I hug the cool porcelain.

Fuck me. How did I get here? Not *here* here, but in life. I had so many hopes and dreams as a kid. Always thinking about the greatness that awaited me when I was a grown-up. If ten-year-old me could see me now... I'm fucking pathetic.

I've fucked up literally every good thing in my life. I'm closer to forty than thirty and have jack shit to show for it except a long line of conquests that I hardly remember and what I'm sure is a wasteland of organs from all the years of numbing my problems.

Every woman I've ever loved has left me. To be fair, that list is comprised of only two and a half names. My ex-wife Melanie gets the half. I never truly loved her. No, that emotion was saved for my first love, Dani, and what I thought would be my forever love, Charlotte.

When we were teenagers, deep in our first love bubble, Dani and I found my dad sticking his dick where it didn't belong—inside her mom.

Yeah, life pretty much rolled straight into the shitter after that.

Dani and her dad moved to Tennessee, and she refused to speak to me again. My folks moved us to Alaska, where I met Charlotte and finished out high school. She turned my world upside down and back again.

But as usual, I fucked it all up.

Now, Charlotte is married to the guy she dated right before me, and I haven't the foggiest about Dani. But I bet she's living out her picket-fence dream with some doting schmuck who still has a dime left to his name.

Not that I blame them at all, but my family cut me off long ago. I grew up pretty privileged as far as wealth goes. Papaw and Mee-maw were the last to sever ties with me. After my second... or no, wait, third DUI and subsequent arrest.

I blearily remember it like it was yesterday.

"Morris, you know the drill. Make your call. You have five minutes." Officer Blart hollers at me while patting his jelly-doughnut-filled belly. His name isn't really Blart, but he reminds

me of that security guy in that one movie.

I sigh heavily as I roll off of the cot in the holding cell and drag myself over to his desk to make a call. The only call I can.

"Hello?" A deep, sleepy voice says over the line.

"Papaw! How the hell are you? Listen man, I'm sorry for waking you up and whatnot, but I'm in a little bit of a jam."

He clears his throat, and I hear the tinkling of an ice cube as he swirls his glass of whiskey in his hand.

Lord, I'd kill for some of the 1926 Macallan he gifted me when I married my first wife, Bex. Though I don't really count that crazy bitch in my matrimonial tally. She drugged me. Tricked me into fucking her by pretending to be my actual girlfriend, Charlotte, and then convinced me I knocked her up. My influential and image-concerned family forced me into a shotgun wedding. After it all came crashing down and ruined my fucking life, it turned out the baby wasn't even mine. I had the marriage annulled and haven't seen the cunt since.

"When are you not in a 'jam' these days, Zachariah?" he asks in a gruff, no-bull-shit tone. Before I can respond, he cuts off any excuses I can muster up. "I told you when you got in the last 'jam' that I wouldn't be stepping in again. You need help son, and I don't know how to give it to you."

I run a hand through my matted and sweat-soaked locks, gripping the roots tightly as I try desperately to keep my anger in check. This man is my fucking blood, and he's acting like we're nothing. Like I'm just so easy to toss aside.

My teeth grind together as if they can keep the fire behind my words at bay, and I tell him what he wants to hear. "I know Papaw. I'm ready to turn it all around. You'll see. I just need you to bail me out and float me some cash—" His deep sigh fills the line, and he cuts off my bullshit. "No, son. It's time you learn some real consequences for your actions. I love you, Zachariah, but we can't keep watching you self-destruct. This is for your own good. I hope one day you see that. I won't be taking your calls again." And just like that, everyone I've ever had in my corner disappeared. And with them, my sense of self-preservation.

My stomach has finally realized there is nothing left to purge. My slick forehead meets the cool porcelain, and as I stare at the regurgitated remains of my innards, I realize this is where I'm supposed to be.

All the choices I've made in life have culminated in this moment.

Broken.

Sick.

Lost.

Powerless.

Chapter 2

Step 2: Came to believe that a power greater than ourselves could restore us to sanity

My feet shuffle lifelessly in my facility-issued slippers as I make my way down the tiled hallway. It's been eight days since I self-admitted to rehab, and today is the first day I didn't wake with quakes so deep in my bones it rattled my brain. I've spent the last 192 hours waiting for death. I was certain it was coming. At times, I prayed for it, too.

"Mr. Morris, looking well today. Can we expect to see you in group?" A far too energetic staff member, Ethan, singsongs at me as I pass his desk.

I fight off a grimace and give him a slight nod. Not stopping for more pleasantries, I make my way into the small cafeteria. The room is filled with circular tables, reminiscent of the accommodations of my elementary school. I plop my body into the closest plastic chair and drop my forehead to the surface.

I'm not sure how much time passes when metal scraping fills my ears and a warm body sits beside me. I don't look up or move at all, waiting for my new table mate to either say something or leave me the fuck alone.

"Mr. Morris. It's been a long time." A gruff but professional voice rings out from my right. It takes my cloudy mind a beat too long to recognize it. But when I do, my irritation burns red hot.

"Oh, goody. It's the predatory therapist. Lemme ask you something, Doc. You kissed anybody's girlfriend today?" My head jolts up, and I sneer at him. My vision blurs with the movement, but I try feverishly to keep my eyes locked on his.

Jensen Turner. The therapist who took advantage of my high school girlfriend. Well, that's how I see it anyway. Charlotte was in a really bad way back then. Not only was she fighting for her life to get off of drugs and treat her depression, but then the sack of shit who had abused her in the most depraved ways, Priest, was killed right in front of us.

He thought I didn't know. He probably thought Charlotte wouldn't say anything to anyone about her trusted therapist cornering her in his car and kissing her. Yeah, she might've been over 18 and had kissed him back, but it's still fucked up in so many ways. We've been broken up for well over 15 years now, and it still burns my ass to think about it.

A kaleidoscope of memories makes its way to my optic nerve. I watch them play out in front of me like an old drive-in movie on fast-forward. *Long blonde hair. Melted chocolate eyes. A dusting of light freckles kissing her heart-shaped face. I love you's. I want to marry you's. I'm yours forever. I never want to see you again. Broken hearts. Broken minds. Lost souls.*

I have only three real regrets in my life.

1. Accepting that drugged cookie from Bex.
2. Hurting Charlotte.
3. Letting Dani walk out of my life forever.

Everything else I've done in my past has served some kind of purpose or lesson. But not those three. What I wouldn't give to go back. While for the majority of my life, I've focused on if I could go back, I would fix things with Charlotte. Or, at the very least, not fuck the whole thing up like I did. But seeing her now? How happy and stable she is with that Gothic dude... I love her too much to ever take that away from her.

No. Now, when I think about going back, I wish to go back to that day in 2004. The day my heart splintered apart for the first time. We were kids. We had no business getting involved in the infidelity of our parents and the subsequent destruction of our lives. Why did *we* have to suffer on top of everything else?

I promise myself right here and now. If I make it through these next 81 days, I will look Dani up and see how her life has unfolded. Was she truly better off without me? Am I destined to be alone? Do I deserve anything but to rot in the solitude of my own making?

Fate. I'll leave it up to fate. Clearly, I've done nothing but fuck my life into the dirt, time after time. It's time to let someone else take the wheel.

Dr. Turner spits a sip of his coffee out across the table at my words. Dabbling his chin with a napkin, he lowers his brow and voice when he responds. "It wasn't like that, Mr. Morris. We made a mistake. We both acknowledged it and moved on. Now, we are great friends and colleagues."

"Well, whoop-de-doo for y'all. Glad you're out here living your best life while I'm stuck in a cage wishing for death most days." I reply sarcastically.

Dr. Turner gives me a pointed look. Okay, I get it. I'm behaving like a childish asshole. That was a lifetime ago, and she hasn't been mine in a long, long time. But still, I have no desire to speak to this man. Call me petty if you want. Fuck him.

He sighs and stands. He taps two fingers on the surface of the table. "You and I have an appointment for a one-on-one tomorrow at noon. See you then."

It takes everything in me not to give him a middle finger salute as he walks away.

I signed up for this, and I have to be willing to do what it takes. I don't want to live this life anymore. I can't. I won't survive it.

Chapter 3

Step 3: Made a decision to turn our will and our lives over to our higher power

Holy shit. Thirty days. Thirty goddamn days.

I think the last time I went thirty days being completely sober was when I was a pre-teen and didn't even have hair on my peaches yet.

Part of me feels guilty for being proud of myself. On one hand, I put in the work. No one can force lasting sobriety on someone else— well, unless they are doing nefarious things like kidnapping and light bondage. Damn, that sounds like a pretty cool time. *Focus, Zach.*

On the other hand, I feel so damn foolish for being in this position in the first place. I've spent more time falling off the wagon than not. I'm not sure how to navigate life with all the sharp edges.

Blurry shapes, uncertain steps, dulled senses... I can do all of that. But the pointedness of reality is almost too much to bear.

I've really cemented my stubbornness with therapy while I've been here. Group and individual. I participate just enough that no one can say I'm not, but never enough to really get anything from it.

The whole concept of putting my life in God's hands is… unsettling. I'm sure the big guy has many better things to do than piece back together the broken shards of my liquor-soaked soul.

I'm not sure what I believe. There are so many theories to subscribe to. Certainly, they can't all be right. So, which God is *the* one? Is it the merciful one? The vengeful one? The judgmental one? The one who promises shit tons of virgins at the pearly gates? The one with all the arms? Hell, my roomie even prays to the porcelain one all too often.

Is this what an existential crisis looks like? Why do I have to believe in some ghost story that's been the world's longest game of "Telephone" ever? Are we really supposed to believe that Peter's cousin's, uncle's, baby sister's, old roommate's, great-granddaddy twelve times removed got the story right? Highly unlikely.

I'm sitting in Dr. Turner's office for the umpteenth time, and like all the times before, I don't have anything to say to the man— until a question strikes me, and I speak it aloud before I can stop myself. "Do you believe in God, Dr. Turner?"

He lowers the novel he was lost in onto his desk, removes the reading glasses from the tip of his nose, and regards me while he ponders his answer. "I believe in a higher power, I suppose. Not necessarily 'God'."

"What's the difference?" I ask as I lay down on my lap the latest model of paper airplane I was working on.

He clears his throat and gives me his full attention. "A higher power is anything outside of yourself, Mr. Morris. It can be God, sure. But it could also be a fully restored Brewster SB2A Buccaneer."

"A what?"

Dr. Turner chuckles and gestures to the crumpled attempt at an aircraft on my thighs. "It's a bomber plane from WW2. It's not important. What I'm trying to get at is your higher power can be whoever or whatever you want or need it to be."

I nod and run my tongue along my front teeth as I let that information sink in. Fucking hell, I want to hate the man, but he's kinda cool. My eyes roll on their own at the realization.

Dr. Turner stands, adjusting his slacks before placing his hands in their pockets. "I am going to be out of the office for the next three weeks. I will have another qualified colleague fill in for my patients during that time. I want to make sure that's not going to be a conflict for you, and if it is, we need to discuss other arrangements."

My nose crinkles, and I cock my head to the side. "Why would I have an objection to whatever shrink comes in next?"

"Well, you are familiar with this particular colleague. Extremely familiar—"

Oh shit, he means...

"Charlie?" I ask, but the question wasn't necessary. Of course, it's Charlie.

"Yes. Dr. Donovan will be filling in for me. Is that an issue for you?" He poses the question with genuine care and concern. It irritates me. Smug fuck. *Oh, look at me, Mr. Tall, Dark and Handsome, with my great career, perfect teeth, and bags of money.* Prick. Finally, I shake my head at him. "Everything's peachy, Doc."

He quirks a brow, seeming to give me an additional opportunity to back out. But I don't. How bad could it be to see the woman I was madly in love with for most of my life, who is now living her best one without me? How terrible would it be to have her see me at the lowest point of my life? Fuck. Can I do this?

Yes. No. Fuck.

"If you say so, I trust that you will let me know if you feel uncomfortable with the arrangements. I will inform Dr. Donovan that she is approved to take over your case in the interim."

I blow out a long breath and stand. I need to get the hell out of here and freak the fuck out in the privacy of my own room. "Okie-dokie, artichokie."

We both pull disgusted faces with my choice of words. I shake my head dismissively. "I don't know why I said that. I've never said those words in my life. See ya later, Doc."

As I spin toward the door, he calls after me. "Oh, Mr. Morris?"

"Yeah?"

He tips his chin up at me as he tosses something in my direction. My football skills slide back into place like muscle memory. I palm the small, round object, feeling its cool metal against my skin. "Thirty days is a big accomplishment. Be proud of yourself. I know I am. One day at a time adds up, Mr. Morris. I'm grateful to be watching you become the man I always knew you could be. Keep up the great work."

A lump forms in my throat as I swallow down the last small shred of pride I desperately hang on to, and I offer him a real smile. "Thanks, man. I appreciate that. Truly."

He responds with a smile and picks up his novel, effectively ending the conversation. I exit his office, closing the door behind me. My heart races as I open my palm flat and expose the bronze medallion. Thirty days. Hell, I just may be able to do this.

Now, to the biggest hurdle of my sober journey so far... what the fuck do I say to Little Bit?

Chapter 4

Step 4: Made a searching and fearless moral inventory of ourselves

I wish I had something better to wear than this bland-ass sea-foam green sweat suit. Like I don't feel emasculated enough on a daily basis in this place. Now I have to see a very important person from my past in this grungy getup.

My hands brace each side of the sink as I stare at my gaunt reflection. The withdrawal symptoms come and go. I'm told that could last for a while and then some. While it's sometimes psychosomatic, the aches and pains are very real.

What will she see when she looks at me? Will she see the charming teenage boy who loved to make her laugh? Or will she see the sad excuse for a man hanging his head at her dorm room entrance as I confirm her worst fear— that I, in fact, cheated on her?

My stomach lurches, and I thrust myself over the toilet just as the remnants of my breakfast make a reappearance.

Great. Just fucking great.

* * *

My hand remains frozen in midair. Poised to knock on the solid wood. *Just do it. Knock. Stop being a pussy. Do it. Now. You're being a little bitch.* I berate myself for my cowardice. My shoulders snap in place, filled with false bravado and determination. Just as I bring my fist, a little too aggressively, to the door, it swings open, and my fist stops millimeters from Charlotte's face.

Her big, chocolate-brown eyes widen in surprise. I stand, paralyzed. Finally, she chuckles, wraps her delicate fingers around my wrist, and pulls my fist down to my side. I simply stare at her. Eventually, she rolls her eyes— such a Little Bit thing to do— and opens her arm with a flourish into the room. I take her subtle cue and make my way to the chair.

"How has the program been for you so far, Mr. Morris?" she asks.

I quirk my brow at her in challenge, which she returns with equal provocation. A snort of laughter flows from me. "Are we gonna pretend that I don't have the taste of you locked up safely in my memory bank, Little Bit?"

She may be a fancy-pants doctor now. But my sassy girl is still there, just with a more bougie wardrobe. Speaking of ass... hers looks fucking fantastic in her leather pencil skirt. My eyes follow the beat of her hips as they sway on the return to her chair. My dick damn near cries in protest when her lower half is cut off from view by the desk.

"Eyes up top, Morris." Charlotte bites out playfully as she glares at my clear gawking. She snaps while pointing to her face. "It's good to see you, Zach. Last time..."

She doesn't need to finish that sentence. We both know how the last time went. I had just gotten yet another DUI and was sent to Aurora North for evaluation. Imagine my surprise when the person I was meeting with happened to be my high school girlfriend that I hadn't seen in a decade and a half.

We were both pretty shocked to see each other. I learned she married her first love. That she believed I was sexually assaulted by Bex in college and hadn't actually "cheated" on her. We hashed out our grievances, and she offered me a way out of the path I was heading down—prison or death. Complete the 90-day rehab program and get clean. So here I am, walking the walk.

"Yeah. You, too." I nod along and offer her a small grin. I don't know what it is about this woman, but every time I see her or, hell, even think about her, it sends me straight back into that teen boy mindset.

"So…?" she asks, and momentarily, I'm confused. That's right. She asked me a question while I was eye-fucking her.

"Well. I'm alive. I'm sober. And I'm super fucking horny… so! Guess it's going good? My right forearm has never been in better shape." I grin at her with a wink. Charlie stares back, straight through me. She's not sucked into my bullshit. She's always been the one to see past the facade.

"Why do you do that, Zach?"

"Do what?"

Her hand motions up and down the length of me. "Hide behind the charm. You don't need to do that with me. You know that. At least, I hope you do."

My smile fades immediately. I do know that. But it's been a long, *long* time since I felt safe enough to do so. The last time I did was with her. Even my best friend, Morgan, hasn't seen me quite as raw as this woman has.

"Can we just be Charlie and Zach for a while?" she asks, her voice small. More meek than I ever want to hear it. Fuck, she doesn't know how badly I want that. I lost her as a lover, but I never wanted to lose her as a friend.

I nod softly and reach my hand out to take hers. "Yeah, sweetheart. We can just be Charlie and Zach."

"So, tell me, really. How are you?"

I give her a small squeeze before pulling my hand back and running it through my dirty blonde hair. "I'm... existing?"

Charlie nods and seems to know exactly what I mean. She's been here before, in my exact shoes. She went through rehab and got clean many years ago. I watched her crash into rock bottom and claw her way back out. She's so damn strong. I wish I had an ounce of her determination and strength. But she's right. I hide. I stuff any realness way deep down and bring out the good-time-fun-guy for the world to see.

"It gets easier. I know it doesn't seem like it right now. But it does. I'm so proud of you. This shit is rough."

Pulling at a loose thread in the cuff of my sweatshirt, I ask. "Does the anger go away?"

Charlie lets out a hearty laugh and slouches back in her chair. "For some people, I'm sure it does."

"What about for people like us?" I press.

She motions back and forth between us with her hand. "People like us? We have hellfire in our veins. But, we find better ways to channel it."

"Like BDSM?" I wink, and she throws a pencil from her desk at me.

"Joke if you must, but actually, BDSM can be a very liberating and healthy experience."

My jaw damn near clashes to the floor. She says that like she knows, *personally*. Damn. My Little Bit has gotten kinky since college. Good for her. Good for that husband of hers, too. Fuck, now I'm back to being jealous of that D-bag.

"I want to be better, Charlie. You know, I think we crossed paths for a reason all these years later. Because you're supposed to be the person to walk down this path with me, and I can think of no better person to be by my side."

She offers me a sweet smile, and it lights me up inside. And because I'm me, I just can't help myself. "But baby, if you'd rather be on top of me instead of the side, I'd be down for that too."

Charlie scoffs, flips me off, and tips her chin to the door. "Boy, bye."

I laugh and open the door, turning back to her. "See you next week, Doc?"

"If you're lucky," she sasses back.

"There she is."

Chapter 5

Step 5: Admitted to our higher power, to ourselves, and to another human being the exact nature of our wrongs

"What's your number?" Charlie asks as she pops an M&M into the air and darts her head to the side to catch it in her mouth.

"My football number? You know that, it's 10. Or do you mean my phone number? It actually hasn't changed since college. Or wait, did you want the number of pounds I can deadlift? It's 320 lbs, by the way."

"That's all fascinating information, but you know what I mean," she snarks in between tosses of M&Ms.

A deep sigh lets loose from my chest. "I don't know."

"You don't know because there's too many to count? Or because you were hammered during the encounters?"

"Yes."

Where I would expect sarcasm, judgment, or anger from any normal person, Charlie simply gets it. Gets me. "Okay."

"Okay? That's all? No calling me a skeeze or whatever manwhores are referred to these days?"

She shrugs a shoulder and tosses another M&M in her mouth, talking around it. "I've been in your shoes, Zach. My skeletons are far from innocent. The things we do while in active addiction are what I like to refer to as my bad brain's doing, 'Ursula'. She did all the bad shit and left me with the consequences."

"Ursula, hmm?" I tease.

"What? You know I like *Friends*, and Phoebe's evil twin sounded like a perfect example of my bad brain. She was a porn star, you know?"

"*Lord*, do I know. You only made me watch that shit on repeat most nights. I'm surprised you aren't president of their fan club." I grouse and throw a piece of my popcorn at her.

She flicks it back to me from across her desk. "Who says I'm not?"

We laugh, and it's so surprisingly simple. How we just fall back into comfort. Home. Safe. Protected.

* * *

The empty side of my room reminds me that this won't last forever. Harrison was discharged. Healed or whatever. Let go to spread his wings and the word of sobriety... this shit kinda feels just a tad like a cult.

Now the bed is empty. Waiting for the next poor body to soil it. Wicking themselves of their choice of numbness and bad decisions.

Having experienced indoc myself, I now understand why Harrison set up the space the way he did. He made sure there was a clear path to the bathroom and had taken the bed furthest away from it. All his personal items were snugly pushed between his bed and the wall, and there was an abundance of towels in the shared bathroom. I heeded his unspoken warning and did the same—just in time for the knock at the door.

"Hello? Zach, it's Ethan. I have someone to introduce you to. This is Mitch." Ethan says cheerily as he enters the room. A twitchy, skinny man with sunken eyes and sores all over his visible skin follows behind him. Twitchy Mitchy.

I nod my head and watch them move around the room. Twitch won't make eye contact with either of us, but that's not surprising.

Once Ethan is satisfied that he's done his due diligence, he leaves the two of us to get "acquainted".

"What's up, man? My name is Zach. Let me know if you need anything. I'm gonna head to group. So you can just settle in and familiarize yourself with the room. I'll be back after a while."

He says nothing and doesn't acknowledge my words in the slightest. Whatever, I did my neighborly duty. I'm not this guy's babysitter.

I make my way to the large, open common room, where we have a group meeting every evening. I participate on occasion when I feel like flaying my wounds open for others to see. But often, I sit and observe, soaking in the stories of those around me. Sometimes, all it takes is to hear about someone with worse deeds than you or who has a deeper sin closet to make you see that maybe you will be okay after all.

We are doing step work today.

Step 5: Admitted to our higher power, to ourselves, and to another human being the exact nature of our wrongs.

Well, shit. This is not the place I want to open that can of worms. Charlie has become my higher power. The person outside of myself that I trust implicitly with my secrets as well as my well-being. And boy, do I have a lot of secrets. *And* that's just the shit I kinda remember. Who knows what fuckery lies deep beneath the surface of remembrance.

After an hour of hearing other people's misdeeds, I'm busting at the seams to have my one-on-one with Little Bit. She asked me not to call her by her nickname anymore. Something about it being unprofessional and hurtful to her husband. But fuck a whole bunch of that. She was, is, and will always be my Little Bit— even if I don't get to see her "bits" anymore.

I've put a Herculean effort into not picturing her naked with my dick buried balls deep inside of her on top of her desk. I've ignored her signature scent of vanilla and sugar. Hell, I've even tried to stop flirting with her. *Tried.* Sometimes. Okay, not really. No red-blooded vagina lover on the planet could resist seeing that sexy flush come over her visible skin when she gets flustered.

I head back to my room, where I find my newest roommate puking his guts out in the shared bathroom. Not surprising. Twitchy Mitchy turns and glares at me when I close the door, so I swallow my words of concern and get ready for bed. He can suffer alone if he's gonna be a dick about it.

I've gotten all too used to sleeping with various obscene noises around me. Instead of counting sheep, I try to count my wrongdoings. But I lost track of the ones that happened after I dropped out of college before drifting off to sleep.

Damn, Little Bit's gonna have her work cut out with me.

Chapter 6

Step 6: Were entirely ready to have our higher power remove all these defects of character

"You know, step work isn't a race, Zach," Charlie says from her perch on the desk, looking down on me.

"I'm not trying to race anybody, LB. I just want to get as much out of this experience as I can before my ninety is up."

"And, when is that?" she questions while uncrossing her legs to throw the right one over the left. I don't even try to peek up her skirt. Look at me: progress!

"In ten days," I respond.

She nods. She knew that already.

I really am not trying to race against anyone or anything. What I told her is the truth. She is the easiest person for me to open up to. She always has been. When my time here is up, so is my time with her.

Last week, we covered as many of my misdeeds as I could recall. I'll give it to her. She never looked disgusted or disappointed in me. And there was some rough shit that came out.

I've slept with countless women. I've cheated. I've lied. I've stolen. Pretty much broke every commandment. Adultery. Coveting. All the things — except murder. Not that I haven't thought about it.

"Ten days may seem like an eternity in here, but it'll come quicker than you expect. What have you done to prep for life on the outside?" Charlie asks thoughtfully. I love that after everything we've been through, separately and together, that we can still be us.

I smile meekly at her. "Not much. I've been taking it day by day, you know?"

She gives me a look. *That* look. The one that says what the ever-loving shit Zachariah? "Okay... well, that's not exactly what you're supposed to take from 'one day at a time'. You need to have a plan. Where are you staying? Who are you staying with? Where will you attend meetings? How will you protect your sobriety? Things can't just go back to how they were before. If you want my advice? Don't stay with your parents or anyone else who could be an emotional trigger for you."

"I never thought that far ahead. If I'm honest, I wasn't sure there would be an 'after' for me..." It's morbid but true. I never thought I'd be alive at this age. I was sure I would've kicked the bucket by now, or somebody would've knocked it out from under me.

A tear forms in Charlie's deep brown eyes. They are sparkling for the wrong reason, and that still guts me to see. She crosses the room and jerks me up by the arm. When we stand toe-to-toe, she grips my cheeks between her palms and locks our eyes together. "You listen to me, Zachariah Thaddeus Morris, you are worthy. You are strong. You are brave. This is one of the hardest things to do, and look at yourself; you're doing it! I am so proud of you and the man you are becoming. There is a long 'after' after this waiting for you."

Before I can stop myself, I wrap her up tightly in my arms and bury my face in her neck. It's like she rips the emotion right out of me. My tears soak into her baby-blue blouse, but she doesn't seem to care. She holds me just as tightly.

Reluctantly, she pulls back. "I've told you a little about Ellie's House, right?"

"The foundation you started to help people over nineteen to get back on their feet? Yeah, a little."

"Well, if you'd like, I have a room for you. There are rules, but you have a safe place to lay your head and three good meals a day. What do you think?" she asks earnestly.

I give her my real smile, the one reserved for her, and nod slowly. "I think I'd be a fool to turn it down. And I'm tired of being a fool. I really appreciate everything you've done for me, LB. I can't thank you enough."

"All I want is for you to finally get to enjoy your life, Zach. That's all I've ever wanted for you. You deserve butterflies and rainbows. You just need to be sober enough to notice it when it's in front of you." She jokes and pats my arm.

"Right. Sure. I'm thinking it's probably best if Rosy Palms and I stick together for the time being."

"Okay. But at least start switching hands. You're gonna look like Popeye before too long. Now get outta here." Charlie winks and waves me out of her office.

When I get back to my room, Twitchy Mitchy is already asleep and sweating through every piece of linen in our room. The stench is almost unbearable. I head to the bathroom and grab my deodorant. Swiping my finger across the top of the stick, I gather a small amount of the gel and rub it just under my nose.

With the stench temporarily handled, I grab my notebook and begin listing the things Charlie and I discussed about my shortcomings.

Thoroughly depressed after listing as many as I could, I throw the notebook across the bed and lay back to try for a little bit of rest.

* * *

I don't know that I've ever just sat alone with my thoughts. Only hearing my own breathing. No background noises or distractions. Just me and the scariest place for me to be: with myself.

I've spent my 36 years on this planet being one type of person. The charmer, the flirt, the good guy. That last one is a little subjective as I'm sure all of my exes would disagree. I don't know how to be myself. I'm not even sure what that really means.

Who am I? What parts of me are carefully curated to fool those around me, and what parts are truly me?

Little Bit was right when she said I mask my feelings with charm. I try to think how far back I can remember putting that mask on...

"Shug, your daddy's going to be here any moment. Did you straighten up your room like I asked?" Mama asks while moving her favorite vases just a pinch to the left or right. Scooping up imaginary dust and debris that don't exist.

All I wanna do is go meet Dani and ride our bikes. Last week, when we went down to the creek that we weren't supposed to go near, we thought we saw a dead body. Dani screamed, and I wanted to poke it with a stick to see if it moved, but she tore off like a bat outta hell, and I had to pedal my legs off to catch up to her. I'm chomping at the bit to see if it's still there and if it's a corpse or not.

I sigh, "Yes, Mama. My room is clean. I picked up all around the house to make sure it was presentable. You know, Daddy is aware that people live here, right? Just cause he's been gone forever doesn't mean he forgot."

Mama bristles and pins me with a stern stare, complete with her hands on both hips. "Don't you talk back to me, Zachariah. I don't ask a lot from you, so when I do, I expect no sass from you about it. You got me?"

I nod and kick my foot at a piece of imaginary debris. "Yes, ma'am."

A loud slam shocks us both out of our stare-down. A shoe comes flying down the hallway.

"Damn it. What kind of pigsty are y'all living in?" Daddy's loud, angry grumble carries to us in the kitchen, and the hairs on the back of my neck stand up. "Zachariah! Get your ass out here and pick up your damn shoes. If I trip over them again, you'll lose every pair you got."

Mama's warm arms come around my shoulders as she whispers in my ear. "Go on and head back to your room, Shug. I'm sure your daddy is just real tired from the international travel."

That was the first time I realized that the daddy who left on deployment was not the daddy who came back. Since I was the "man of the house" while he was gone— and it was often— it was up to me to keep Mama safe and happy.

And the mask was born.

Chapter 7

Step 7: Humbly asked our higher power to remove our shortcomings

Staring down at the lined paper before me, I realize I don't have a great answer for Charlie's questions.

1. What do I get emotionally from an abundance of casual sex?
2. Why do I need alcohol to numb myself to the point of being able to go through with it?
3. Why do I feel the need to have all females around me find me desirable?
4. How do I feel afterward?
5. How much of what the women felt mattered to me?

Damn, dude.

If I didn't feel like a giant piece of shit before, I certainly do now. Because, honestly? I couldn't give a shit less what my partner of the minute wanted, needed or felt. As long as the consent and warm pussy was there, it was a done deal.

Why did I need substances to get through it? It wasn't like it was a necessity, but as long as I was blitzed out of my mind,

I could pretend a multitude of things to be the truth. Any blonde could turn into Charlie. Any brunette could turn into Dani. Any moans could be a taut supermodel giving me her best performance.

It makes me feel… needed.

Why do I feel like I need to be needed?

Am I really out to be Captain Save-A-Hoe, as LB so delicately put it?

Irritated with my own shitty existence, I hurl my pen at the wall and flop back on my bed. Staring at the ceiling, hoping the answers will become clear. That somehow, I will magically be a better man.

If only it worked that way.

* * *

I barely tap the wood of the door before opening it with a flourish. "Honey, I'm ho—" My words falter when the person behind the desk is not my favorite blonde but instead is a grumpy-faced, middle-aged dude who could give George Clooney a run for his money. Fucker.

"Mr. Morris, it's great to see you in such good spirits. Come on in," Dr. Turner says, removing his spectacles from his bridge and smiling politely. The original scowly nature of his sharp jaw fades instantly. Maybe Dr. Turner wears a mask, too?

I glance around the office, dipping my head in different directions like she might be hiding under a piece of furniture.

"Dr. Donovan has gone back to her own patients with my arrival back at the facility. Don't worry, I have her notes, and I'm more than happy to pick up where she left off with your treatment plan."

No.

I don't want this dick. I want Charlie. Charlie knows me. Charlie understands me. Charlie has been with me through the start of my end.

My head shakes as my thoughts rattle around. Dr. Turner senses my hesitation immediately. "Mr. Morris— Zach, I know you and Charlie have a certain... history. And you probably feel very comfortable with her. Can I offer a different perspective? If you don't at least see my point of view, I will concede, and you may skip one-on-ones for these next 6 days of your treatment."

I eye him suspiciously before shrugging because why not? Worse case? I get to skip seeing his stupid face for the duration.

"Comfort is great for opening the locks of our souls. It gives us the boost we need to find the courage to face the darkest paths behind us. But do you know what comfort doesn't offer? Change."

It feels like he just judo-punched me in the chest.

"Change is what we strive for in our own patterns and behaviors. Do you know what the definition of insanity is, Zach?" he asks, and I don't miss that he's dropped the formality of the Mr. Morris business.

I nod.

"Tell me, please." Dr. Turner urges.

"Doing the same thing over and over and expecting different results," I answer.

"And what's another way to say that that you've learned during your time here?"

"Nothing changes if nothing changes," I say with finality. Fuck me. He makes sense. *Goddammit!*

I don't want to like this guy. Yes, I'm trying to grow as a person and be better and blah blah... but I'd like to just keep my grudge against this guy. Can't I just hold one teeny, tiny, little petty grudge?

A wide smile breaks over his face, showcasing those perfectly straight pearly whites. "You're going to be alright, Zach."

Shit. Why did that feel so good to hear? Was it just the words in general? Or was it the person giving them?

Hold the fucking phone. Am I equating Dr. Turner to my dad? Is that why I try to hate his guts so much?

Ho-ly shit.

Maybe I'm on the way to becoming a better man after all...

Chapter 8

Step 8: Made a list of all persons we had harmed, and became willing to make amends to them all

As much as I'd love to declare from the rooftops that Zach Morris is a graduate of the ninety-day rehab program and is the best version of himself... I still have a long way to go.

But I have a starting point and people in my corner cheering me on. For the first time in a long time, I have hope.

Hope for a better future. Hope for a better me. Hope for change.

A loud honk breaks me from my thoughts. A busted old Camry pulls up and screeches to a halt before me. The clunker shimmies and shakes as its driver reaches over to the passenger window and cranks it down.

Max Mother-Fucking Whitaker. One of the only friends I have left from my days at River View High.

"Morris! You beautiful bastard, you heading my way?" Maxi chuckles, and I open the very squeaky door and climb my big ass into the tiny sedan.

"Oh, Maxi Pad, you know I'm always going your way." I slap a hand on his shoulder and give him a wink.

Maxi smiles brightly, and his eyes turn a bit glassy. "Dude. I missed you."

As much as I want to give him shit and call him a pussy for getting all emotional on me, I don't. Because, fuck, I missed him, too.

"We can get all in our feels and paint each other's nails as soon as you get some food in my stomach. I feel like I haven't had a decent meal in— well, at least 90 days."

"You got it, Cap'n." He still calls me that even though we are in our mid-thirties and high school football was a lifetime ago. It makes me smile. Maxi is one thing I hope never changes.

"Where you wanna grab grub from?" he asks as we pull onto the busy main street of River View.

We lock eyes momentarily and give our answers at the same time. "Pizza Guy!"

* * *

"Why are you shaking the whole ass place, bro?" Maxi asks with a mouth full of his BBQ Chicken pizza.

I didn't realize I was. I don't know why I'm so nervous. I've seen her many times now since we... reconnected. But this will be the first time outside of a clinical setting since the reunion that I barely remember.

I have patches of memory of the night. I was getting dome from some random chick in the bathroom, and she walked in while I was snorting a line. But the sight of her luscious mouth popping open in shock sent me over the edge. I came so hard and not for the nameless curly-headed bimbo on her knees. I said some horrendous shit, and she started to cry. I think.

Things get a bit hazier after that. I remember Maxi wrapping her in his arms, and I was pissed. Like I had any right to be. Hell, my own damn wife was feet away inside the reunion. But Mel was used to my philandering ways. It had always been that way between her and me. I did what I wanted, and she had to choose to grin and bear it or walk away. She liked my money, so she stayed all the way up until I was officially cut off.

I know I said something that got me knocked out. I thought it was her boyfriend, Jason. But it turned out to be a feisty little redhead friend of Charlie's instead. I probably would've been embarrassed if I wasn't so fucked up.

Maxi wolf whistles at something behind me. Parts of his crust fly out of his mouth and land on my plate. "Dude! What the fuck?" I shout, temporarily distracted, so I don't know she's arrived until she leans across the table and kisses Maxi on the cheek.

"Oh, Maxi. Save the charm for your wife." Charlie says in a syrupy, sweet tone before smacking me on the arm with the back of her hand. "Scoot."

I laugh and shimmy over to give her enough space to sit on the bench beside me. Without a second thought, I hold my piece of pizza over to her, and she takes a big bite. "Fuck, I miss carbs." she groans, and Maxi's smile increases tenfold while he gives her a wink. "I hope it all goes to your ass, Charlie."

She flips him off and grabs a slice for herself, sticking her tongue out at him and taking another large bite. "I'll make sure Sharissa knows how you feel about the placement of my body fat."

Maxi's eyes widen in horror. "You shut your dirty mouth and say nothing to my wife about this!" He whispers mock-angrily at her. I can tell these two have gotten closer over the years.

It's funny how things just continue to move on without me. I don't know why I thought everything would be frozen in time in my absence. Just waiting for me to arrive so it can start again. Sounds kinda narcissistic now that I think about it.

But no, time marches on and waits for no one. The hurt I caused stretched in time, festering into unclosable wounds. How do I come back from that?

Will anyone truly forgive me? How can I expect them to when I don't know that I can even forgive myself?

Chapter 9

**Step 9: Made direct amends to such people wherever possible,
except when to do so would injure them or others**

Ellie's house is nothing like the shithole halfway house I pictured. No, this looks like a sorority house. Inviting entry. Soft lighting along every wall in lightly bronzed sconces. Pale blueish gray painted on every wall. Those walls are all adorned with tasteful art pieces or decor.

It's like someone plucked this house out of a Better Homes & Gardens magazine. Thank Mama for my knowledge of that one.

Hell, the bathrooms even look like they are fit for better asses than mine. Sleek toilets with bidets— I remember those from my grandparents' estate. Back when I was allowed there. I hope to one day earn my spot back amongst the Morris family.

"It's nice, right?" a soft, feminine voice rings out from behind me. I turn to see a small wisp of a girl. Brown hair falls to her shoulders, and her sharp nose is downturned. She drops her gaze immediately to the ground.

I offer her an easy smile, not wanting to put off any intimidating energy and spook her even more. "Yeah, it is. Not what I was expecting at all."

A gentle chuckle escapes her, and she pulls the long sleeves of her top tight down around her hands. Muddy hazel eyes direct my way as she peers up at me shyly. I stealthily take a small step backward, widening the space between us. Her petite form seems to relax. "I'm Sally. Em tasked me with showing you around the house and getting you settled. She'll be by in a few hours to give you all the official information, though."

Em? That must be Emily. Charlie told me about the unofficial "den mother" of the house. A woman who has clawed out of her own hell and has now made it her life's mission to do the same for others. A true bleeding heart type. I admire that.

"I'm—"

"Zach. Yes, I know. Come with me, please." She cuts me off, blurting out the words at a breakneck pace. I bite my cheek to stop the laughter that wants to come out. Sally seems easily embarrassed, and I don't want to make her uncomfortable. So I nod and hold my hand out in the direction of the stairs. "Of course, madam. After you." She lets out a tiny giggle and rolls her eyes but leads the way.

* * *

I don't know when I fell asleep, but this bed has to be the most comfortable shit I've ever had underneath my body. As soon as I fell into it, I was a goner. I probably would've slept the day away if it weren't for the persistent knock at my bedroom door.

Reluctantly, I drag myself out of bed and open the door. A short woman with tan skin and a platinum blonde pixie haircut stands before me. Her eyes run up and down my body. Not in a sexy way. As if calculating whether I'm going to be more hassle than I'm worth kind of way.

"I guess I can see it," Pixie says, her tone bored and borderline irritated. The confusion must read easily on my face because she clarifies her mystery statement. "That she gave you her heart once."

Ah. There's only one "she" that could be in reference to. Not really wanting to take yet another trip down memory lane and all my failures, at least not with this stranger, I clear my throat and introduce myself. "Zach. And you must be the famous Emily."

"You can call me Em. Follow me. I'll give you the official tour and go over the rules of the house. If you have any questions... too bad. This is my domain. What I say goes. You got a problem with it, you can fill out a comment card and stick it up your ass." Em's face is expressionless as she rains sass upon me. I stare back at her, speechless, before busting an absolute gut. One perfectly shaped eyebrow raises, and Em rolls her eyes before spinning around to begin the tour. She thinks I didn't see the slight lifting of the corner of her mouth. Ah, Em. I will wear you down, eventually.

After a brief tour and several rules, I finally got to meet the other residents. Not only am I the oldest one— by far. But I'm also the only guy. Under normal circumstances, a man might be pretty stoked to be the only fox in the hen house. To me? This shit is a fucking nightmare. I'm talking "burned face guy with knives for fingers chasing you into a dark alley with no escape" nightmare.

That's one of the rules of the house I have no problem adhering to: *no fraternization between residents.*

I haven't even rubbed one out in months. My libido must've taken the brunt of the crash into rock bottom and scattered to pieces before perishing in a blaze of shame and booze-soaked memories.

Turns out, when your life has crumbled into the biggest pile of shit, you kinda lose the desire to be around other people. Especially sober.

I no longer have the patience to be the social butterfly I once was. I'm learning to be okay all by myself. God. How am I even going to deal with *people* without something to take the edge off...

Running.

Running is my new drug of choice. I forgot how much I missed it. Some runners feel the need to fill the silence and drown out their thoughts. Not me. I don't run with music. I want to hear my feet pounding against the pavement. The low hum of traffic from main streets close by. Just me and the path forward.

When I was in high school, I ran four miles daily up Sky Ridge and back. The crisscross curves lead up to the breathtaking view of the quaint town of River View. It became one of my favorite places in the world.

My feet carry me to the flat expanse atop the Sky Ridge road. When I reach the barrier of the edge, I suck in a lung full of crisp Alaskan air. The mountain ranges that make up the backdrop seem to go on forever.

The sound of crunching gravel rips my focus away. A completely restored '69 Camaro rumbles its way to the center lot. Instead of the yellow, red, or even blue these classics typically rock up in, this one is pitch black with neon purple racing stripes running down the center of the car.

But what makes me bust out laughing is the music pouring from the deeply thumping bass of the inside. *Everybody* by Backstreet Boys is heard crisp and clear as the driver steps out of the vehicle.

Beat up white Chucks. Ripped jeans. Jagged 80s band tee.

"Step into my office, Mr. Morris," Little Bit says playfully as she skips over to a very familiar wooden picnic table. I follow her over to the graffitied centerpiece of the space.

She climbs up and plops her ass on the table top. My hands run over the carvings from decades of artwork. Some are so faded you couldn't tell if it was supposed to be a skull or toilet bowl.

Charlie is likely responsible for at least 80% of the contributions. This is her most coveted space on the planet. Or it was. I don't really know her nowadays I guess.

"It's not the same one." She says, running her hands over the acronym *ODAAT*. I watch her, loving seeing a smile on her face. "I had the old one, from back in the day, converted into my home office desk. I just couldn't let it go, you know? It's such a big part of my history. Of *our* history."

Nodding my head, I pat her knee, drawing her attention to the motion. She links our fingers together and meets my gaze. Her chocolate brown eyes searching my emerald green ones. "I'm so sorry, LB. I can't even begin to tell you how much."

We've always been on a compatible wavelength. Knowing what the other is thinking with minimal words. I don't feel the need to fill in the silence with tales of my past fuck ups. It's not needed, anyway.

"I know, Zach. I know."

Chapter 10

Step 10: Continued to take personal inventory, and when we were wrong, promptly admitted it

"Say it you blonde-headed fuck!" Em shouts at me, face red and steam practically rolling out of her ears. My eyes roll, and I shake my head at her. No fucking way am I saying it. She couldn't pull the words from my cold, dead voicebox. Nu-uh.

It's been a few months since I moved into Ellie's House. Things have actually gone pretty well. I got a job with the city, doing maintenance and a whole host of other random tasks. It pays okay, but the most important thing is that I feel like I'm contributing to society again. And not by spreading my cum far and wide like Johnny fucking Appleseed.

A rolled-up magazine flies across the table and smacks right into the side of my face. Blinking up in shock, I stare at Em. Did she really just do that? "Grow up, Em." I chide and slide the magazine I refuse to look at back to her.

"Whoa. What is going on in here? Zach, what did you do?" Charlie directs her accusation at me. Like I'm clearly the one to blame for the calamity occurring. I roll my lips together. I'm locked up tighter than Fort Knox, and I'm prepared for a long-lasting standoff of admission.

Em glares at me and flings the magazine into Charlie's chest. She looks down at the cover and then back at the two of us with confusion. "Uh—" she mutters before pursing her lips and ping-ponging her gaze between us.

"He won't say that I'm fucking right. I told him that you know a movie star, and he laughed at me. So I broke out the evidence, and the stubborn asshole still refused to admit it even with clear proof in his stupid face!"

Charlie laughs and pulls out her phone. The chime for a video chat request echoes off the dining room walls. After a few trills, a male voice comes on. "Hello, Darling. You know I love you to bits, but you know I have to be at the studio in—" the voice fades out briefly before coming back. "Three hours!" he whines, and in true Charlie fashion, she gives zero fucks. She points her front-facing camera at my face, and there he fucking is. Reggie Madson. In the drowsy flesh.

"As handsome as this gentleman is, you know I'm a goner for Sariah and always will be." Reggie yawns the words out, his eyes fluttering closed again.

Charlie hollers from across the room as she makes her way back to me. "Thanks, boo, that's all I needed. Sleep well. Give Sariah and Willow my love!" She ends the call without fanfare while I sit dumbstruck.

"How—?" I can't even form a damn sentence.

Em and Charlie glance at each other before turning in tandem to grin at me. "I met Reg when I was in college. We went to the same AA meetings, and I became an extension of his family with his wife, Sariah, and daughter, Willow. I used to run lines with him back when he was just a starving artist. So when he had a plus one for the premiere of his film '*Last Man on the Island*', your girl was his first choice." Charlie punctuates the end of the sentence with a fucking curtsy.

Wow. How much life has changed. At the same time, mine went down the shitter quick, fast, and in a hurry. Charlie has fought and clawed her way to the life she always deserved. Successful career. Rich husband who happens to be her first love. Rubs elbows with the stars. Built the family she always wanted. Philanthropist. Gorgeous. But still has kept her same zest and sass that makes her unequivocally Charlotte.

I hold my hands up in surrender. I know when I'm beat. "Okay. Okay. There might be a small, teeny tiny, microscopic chance that I wasn't entirely correct."

"That's a lot of word salad to say you're wrong, Zach." Charlie jokes, and the three of us fall into an easy conversation. Charlie regales us with a play-by-play of her red carpet experience and other various life events.

"LB, are you fucking serious?" I stare, stunned, at this woman who continues to baffle me day after day. I asked how Charlotte and Emily met and became what they are now— sisters from different misters. They met at the same facility where Charlie had been forced to complete a ninety-day stint. Only it was four years apart, and Em was the patient with Charlie as her Chemical Dependency Counselor.

Em is tough as nails. I figured she didn't have a rosy upbringing, but this woman. Man. She's been through it. Bounced around from foster home to foster home. Abuse. Neglect. Violence. I can see how turning to drugs seemed like the only way out at the time for her.

What I absolutely didn't expect was hearing about the last home Em was in before being placed permanently with Charlie. The fucking bastards. The husband raped her. And when the wife came in later, beat the shit out of Em for being a "whore".

Em called Charlie to pick her up, and the rest is history.

Except for the brief time directly after when Charlie decided to pull a vigilante move and show up at the house with a baseball bat. She spared most of the details, but I do know that for every injury given to Em, the wife received back tenfold.

My mouth drops open as I take in the information. Fuck. It seems like I've been all wrong. Where my Little Bit was a sassy broken beauty, this Charlie is a fucking badass. She's really taken the shit life's handed her and turned it on its head. She's an inspiration. Clearly. All I have to do is look at the people around her. People she's helped for no other reason than they needed it. No ulterior motives. No narcissistic need for praise. Just people helping people.

It gives me hope. One day, I, too, could be a better man.

Chapter 11

Step 11: Sought through prayer and meditation to improve our conscious contact with our higher power as we understood it, praying only for knowledge of its will for us and the power to carry that out

I've always believed in destiny. Fate. Kismet. Whatever you want to call it. I think that you can try to change your path all you want, but if it's truly not what's meant for you, then you'll keep spinning your wheels, getting nowhere.

There's a reason my mama decided to stick with my sperm donor when she found out about his decade-long affair. That ultimately pulled me apart from my first love. But landed me squarely in front of my second love.

There's a reason I loved and lost. It was meant to be. How could I be the man anyone needs when I haven't been able to look myself in the mirror in years? I know what kind of person I've become. A shit one.

I like to think I'm beyond that by now. That I've grown as a person. I've been on the straight and narrow for... ten months, five days, and seven hours— give or take a few minutes.

I'm not so delusional to think it's smooth sailing from here, and the work is behind me. It's going to take day-by-day, hour-by-hour, minute-by-minute steps in the right direction. I never want to be the me from *before.*

I've spent far too much of the precious time we have on this Earth not being present. Exuding selfish behavior and just being an all around total dick. Especially to the female population.

How do I make amends to an entire gender? That's just going to have to go in my "higher power box" — the mental space I hold for atonement of my sins that cannot be rectified to the person it hurt.

After nearly a year since hitting my rock bottom, I finally feel ready. Ready to move forward. Ready to face my demons head-on. Ready to *live.*

I've saved enough money to have a decent down payment on a house. I thought about renting an apartment, but I'm in my manifesting shit era. I want a home. A permanence. Something that's all mine.

* * *

"Usually, we need at least two solid years of paystubs on top of a sizeable down payment, but it seems we will be waving that requirement for you today—" the loan officer eyes me suspiciously from across the expansive desk. Jesus, man. She's acting like this is all coming out of her own personal coffers. Take the stick out of your ass and calm the fuck down. I squint at the nameplate that she moved off to the side to allow for all of the closing documents. *Karen.* Yeah, it fucking figures. "Must be nice to have friends in high places." Karen huffs under her breath.

Two excruciatingly long hours later, I am officially a home-owner. Holy shit. This is the first time in my thirty-six years on the planet that I've felt like an adult. As I stand on *my* front porch, on *my* seven acres, the air just seems sweeter. A gentle lapping of water sounds in the near distance from the small lake in my backyard. That, along with the unobstructed mountain view, was the selling point for me. The house needs some repair and renovation, but that's okay. I'm ready to put in the work.

Deep thumps of bass and screamo overpower the gentle aqueous hum. *Short Stories With Tragic Endings* by From Autumn to Ashes slices through what used to be a calm, relaxing space as the Camaro comes to a halt in front of me.

"You have the weirdest taste in music of anyone I know, LB." I laugh, leaning a shoulder against the pillar between the stairs. Charlie flips me off, like I knew she would, and rummages around her vehicle for a minute before skipping her way to me with arms covered in grocery bags.

"That shit is a fucking hazard." Charlie snorts after almost busting her ass on some loose floorboards on her way to the kitchen. "You should do something about that."

I laugh, taking the rest of the bags off of her arms, and begin to put stuff away. In a very unorganized and displeasing way, if the scowl on her face has anything to say about it. "Well, I know I've owned it for a whole five minutes. It's on the list. For now, it's getting a piece of red tape."

"Red tape?" she asks.

I nod and take a swig from the bottle of OJ before placing it in the fridge. "Yeah, I'm gonna wander about the house, and anything that might be lethal gets a piece of red tape. You know, so I don't die."

"What about when you gotta pee in the middle of the night?"

"Shit." Fuck, I didn't even think about that. "Maybe reflective tape or glow-in-the-dark?"

"Okay, well, while you ponder different ways to stay alive in your haunted lake house... I want to have a housewarming party for you this weekend. But since—" she pauses and gestures wildly with her hand around the room. "Doing it at your house would be like an episode of *Legends of the Hidden Temple*. We'll be doing it at my house."

"Oh, um, I'm not sure about that, LB." My hand wraps around the back of my neck, and I rub at the tension that's suddenly weighing down on me.

Charlie pauses, putting the new dishes in the sink to rinse, and crosses her arms. With a slight cock of her head and a smirk on her mouth, she says, "Oh, my friend, you misunderstand me. It wasn't a question. Next Saturday, 6 PM."

"Yes, ma'am."

Chapter 12

Step 12: Having had a spiritual awakening as the result of these steps, we tried to carry this message to others and to practice these principles in all our affairs

I feel like an adolescent boy going to his first school dance with two left feet and mismatched socks.

This is the first party I will be attending since starting on my sober journey. What do you bring to a party that's full of recovering addicts? Fucking apple juice? Cupcakes? I must've changed my shirt nine times. To be fair, it was with the same three options. Finally, I decided on a plain black tee. Classic. Easy to hide stains. Shit. Maybe I should've put on a little more deodorant. Well, too late now.

I may have double-parked my truck in the Gas ' n ' Go parking lot in my haste to grab my contribution to my housewarming party. This place may not seem like the perfect place to pick up some grub, but I happen to know they make the best blue-motherfucking-raspberry slushie this side of the Mississippi.

Sipping on my very large cup of blue goodness, I wander the aisles. Jerky? Nah, too douche vibes. Doughnuts? Eh, maybe. Chips? I'm sure there will be plenty; that's like the go-to snack for any gathering.

Spinning in a circle, my eyes land on the prize. I grin and sprint over to the cooler. I'm not sure how many people will be there, so I grab every one available. I have to make a couple of trips from the cooler to the counter and back again to get them all.

"Hello sweet thang, hosting a birthday party?" A raspy voice trying just a little too hard to sound like a Valley girl coos from behind the counter.

A coughing fit overtakes her, and my head jerks up in concern. Her hands wave me off. Okay, apparently, this is a common occurrence for her. Maybe someone should tell her to lay off the cigarettes. I know she's a smoker because not only does she smell like a sickly sweet ashtray, but two of her fingers have yellowing nails. Gross.

I shake my head. I don't know why I entertain her question, but I correct her anyway. "Nah, a housewarming party."

Her face wrinkles, and the cakey foundation that's two shades too dark for her creases. She looks vaguely familiar. My eyes creep away from the horror show happening on her face down to her name tag. I can barely make out "Tiffany"; the thing is so faded. "And *this* is what you're bringing? Why not booze like a normal person?"

Cue my internal eye roll. I shouldn't have answered her to begin with. I just want to get the hell out of here. "You know what? It is a birthday party. My niece is turning eight, and there's a gaggle of little girls who will lose their minds when they see what their good ol' Uncle Zach brought."

Tiffany's brows raise, but she doesn't comment. Slowly, way too fucking slowly, she loads the bottles into bags. I can't help but notice the lecherous way her eyes run up and down my body. Vomit starts to creep up my throat. I reach into my pocket to grab my phone, and my hand rubs against the key ring. That gives me an idea.

"That'll be $54 today, handsome. Say, how about you save one of those for me? I get off at 8 PM." She grins, and I'm greeted with the most unsettling shade of yellow across her teeth.

Decision made. I slide the ring over my finger, palming my truck key, and hold up a fist. "Sorry darlin', but I don't think my wife would like that plan. Have a great night." I scoop the bags and take off before she can jump across the counter and have her wicked way with me. There's that vomit again.

* * *

I don't think of myself as a little bitch, but when Charlie's husband, Jason, answered the door, my butt puckered a little bit. We have a similar body type and height, but he's got a darkness in his eyes that I never want to see directed my way.

Wanting to start my amends to Jason, I offer my hand. For a brief moment, I think he's going to burn my olive branch. He finally puts his hand in mine and gives a shake with just a tad too much strength behind it.

I follow him into the house, nodding at Jensen and who I assume is his wife, as we pass them to the kitchen. I lay my bounty on the marble island, alongside the fancy spread of meat, cheese, crackers, and the like.

A gruff chuckle comes from Jason. "Trying to get on her good side, I see. I don't need to worry about you, do I?" Even though the words are enough to stop me in my tracks, there is humor behind them, and that lets me breathe evenly.

I hold my hands up in surrender. "Nothing to worry about here. I just saw them and knew they used to be her favorite. So this is my thank you for all the help she's given me over the last year."

Jason claps his hand against my shoulder. "I'm just giving you shit. She'll love it. Thanks, bud."

Okay, we are doing the "buddy" thing. I can work with this. I'm glad he seems to be open to my presence because I owe him an amends, and there's no time like the present. I peek around the area. I haven't seen Charlie yet.

"She's out on an errand. She should be back within the hour." Jason answers my unasked question. I nod and gather my balls. "Hey man, so I was wondering if we could have a quick chat."

His brow quirks at that. Obviously, we are talking now, but I don't want an audience for the talk I want to have. He seems to understand my hesitation and swipes a bottle of water, pointing it at the sliding glass door. I follow him out to the back patio and let out a low whistle.

A large fire pit in the shape of an octagon is buried partly inground and is the centerpiece of a huge wooden circular structure with six swings attached all around it. Damn. This is some next-level shit. We each commandeer a swing, and he sits in silence, waiting for me to start.

"Look, I have done a lot of shit things in my life. But most of my regrets lie with how things went down with Charlotte. Before, during, and after we dated. And I know the hurt I caused bled into your relationship. The peak of my jackass behavior was certainly in how I behaved at the five-year reunion. I was shit-faced and don't have a crystal clear picture of the night, but I know I crossed many lines. I hurt Charlotte. Again. And said some fucked up shit to you. I'm sorry. I want you to know that I think you are a stand-up guy. And if it wasn't going to be me, I'm glad it's you."

The silence stretches for longer than I'd like, but finally, he clears his throat. "I accept your apology. We don't know each other, but I can tell you are really embracing this part of your life. It's a hard road to travel, and having Charlie in your corner means always having someone get your back, right or wrong. I've been on the other side of hurting her myself. She's a good judge of character with a great soul. If she believes you're alright, then I do, too."

"Fuck, man. You're getting me all misty over here." I wave my hand dramatically at my eyes. Things are getting just a bit too real and serious. I'm grateful we are agreeing to be in a good place with each other. I plan to keep my place in Little Bit's life, and obviously, her husband is a massive part of that.

A commotion stirs in the house, and the sound filters out to us. We stand in tandem and head back inside.

Em, Jensen and wife— I really need to get her name— Savvy and her husband, Asher, are all gathered around the kitchen island. Jason and I insert ourselves. I know it's supposed to be a party for me, but these are Charlie's people. But I do hope to make them my people, too.

"What's good, my party people?" Maxi sing-songs as he strolls through the door with... an ice cream cake? His wife, Sharissa, rolls her eyes as she enters behind him.

We get a good bro hug in and chat about my new place and all my plans. It feels easy being here, comfortable.

The room falls to a hush as Charlie comes in. She makes a beeline for a Yoohoo and winks at me. "You still know me so well, Zach. Fucking love Yoohoo's." She holds the bottle up in a distant cheers, and I return with my water.

I try to get back to my conversation with Maxi, but I can't help but notice Charlie giving me a strange look. I can't quite place it. It's like a smirk mixed with a hint of fear. A very odd pairing, especially for the woman who has no filter.

It would be moments before I found out why.

Those seconds stretched decades as a tap came from behind me. My heart nearly ceases to beat when I look at the person before me. Is this real? My eyes shoot over to Charlie, the uncertainty still hanging between us. Finally, she nods her chin, a silent command to address the woman. A woman I haven't seen since... we were sixteen.

II

Part Two

Life happens when we are busy making other plans
-unknown

Chapter 13

5 weeks ago

Dani

I duck my head as a drinking glass flies in my direction. It narrowly misses me and shatters against the wall. That'll be my fault, too.

"How are you this fucking useless? I swear to Christ you're dumber than that whore mother of yours. Maybe I should've fucked her, instead of you. Would've gotten some decent pussy, at least from the word on the street. But wouldn't have had to put up with the bitch attached to it or deal with the spawn she insisted on popping out." My husband, Greg, snarls at me in accusation from his position at the kitchen counter.

My crime? Falling in love with him freshman year of college and ignoring every blazing red flag that he spotlighted for years.

The change started slowly. A snide comment here. A roll of the eyes there. An "accidental" shove as he barreled past me in the hallway.

Eventually, that turned into daily shoves that were no longer under the guise of accident. What seems like hourly berating rants on all my shortcomings as a wife, mother, human, and overall stain on society.

I wish I could say there was a sudden change, some snap to explain his horrendous behavior. But no. It was so slow in its build-up that when I realized I was in the thick of it, there was no way out.

Greg loves to remind me that I have nothing. Everything is his. He has connections everywhere. I won't survive without him. Fuck, at this point, I won't survive *with* him.

I've done what I've had to do to protect my daughters. My twins. My reason for living. Felicity and Olivia. For their entire eight years on the planet, I've managed to keep the worst of it hidden from them.

A well-placed piece of jewelry to hide the handprint on my neck. A long-sleeve top in the middle of summer to cover bruises along my arms. Heaps of makeup to cover black eyes, split lips, or cuts. Large sunglasses to camouflage swollen eye sockets. Every trick in the battered wife handbook— I've tried them all.

After seventeen years together, I know his triggers. I know when his lid is about to be flipped. This nice big house is also outfitted with many rooms, three stories, and thick walls. On the nights when I can't hold back the screams, I'm thankful for the thick walls.

Gregory Roberts is a valued member of the Appleville Police Department. Public service is in his blood. His father is a retired Captain, his grandfather was a Sheriff, both of his brothers are firefighters, and his niece is an EMT.

Basically, he has eyes and ears everywhere. Nowhere and no one is safe. I'm trapped here, and my only reason to keep going is to get my daughters to safety before he kills me. I've been stashing a little bit of money, very slowly, over the years. I found an old sewing tin with a false bottom at a market once, and that's been my hiding spot. But there's no way I can make a fresh start with eight hundred dollars, and the sand in my hourglass is starting to run thin.

"Fuck this. I'm going out. Clean this shit up and make sure to shower before bed. I might be in the mood to make love to my wife when I return." Greg spits out as he puts on his leather jacket and digs his truck keys out of his pocket. I don't respond. He doesn't care what my response is. Even if it's "no". To Greg, that word means nothing.

I release a shaky breath when I hear the engine roar fading. Falling to my knees, I reach for the larger pieces of glass. The tears falling from my traitorous eyes distort the shards. I vowed long ago not to let this man have any more of me than he already has.

Ouch.

The loud trill of our landline startles me into gripping my hand around the sharp edges. I rush to the kitchen and grab the corded phone, holding it with my shoulder as I rinse my bloodied hand.

"Hello?"

"Hi, may I speak to Dani, please?"

My heart nearly stops in my chest. No one calls me Dani. Not since before college. When I met Greg, he thought it sounded like he was a man who enjoyed the company of other men. He insisted I go by my full name. Danica.

"Hello?" Her voice rings out in the silence.

My mouth opens and closes without releasing sound for one more "hello" from this mystery woman before I snap out of it. Clearing my throat and shutting off the faucet, I finally respond. "This is she. Who is this?"

"Oh, thank God. Remind me to give Jacobs a gift for his

brilliance—" She breathes out a sigh of relief. But my confusion remains abundant. "Don't mind me, I'm just excited he was able to actually find you. My name is Charlotte Johnson, and I have a favor to ask of you..."

Chapter 14

2 weeks ago

Dani

I don't know why I feel so nervous. My heart is racing, and sweat is running down my spine. Gazing down at my wristwatch to check the time, I realize that I'm a little early. The girls will be done with soccer practice in less than an hour. I never leave them on their own for practice. I always make sure they know they have one parent who adores them and would do anything and everything for them.

Appleville is a small town. Leaving a very limited number of places to have a clandestine meeting with a random person who called me out of the blue three weeks ago. The wind was knocked out of me when she told me what and *who* the purpose of her call was.

I didn't want to venture too far from the girls, and Greg checks my location often via our family tracking app. Funnily enough, he's the only one allowed to have the app. I left my phone in the car so it would show us at the field. There's a heavily wooded trail off the side of the parking lot that leads to a Frolf course, which is thankfully empty.

I find myself doing the "mom sway" as I look around anxiously. I don't even know what this woman looks like or anything about her. She could be a crazy ex of Zach's coming to kill me because we lost our virginity to each other. Oh God. My spine snaps straight when I hear the crack of a branch and shuffling of feet.

Thump.

Thump.

Thump.

Bile creeps up my throat moments before I finally gather my courage to spin around. A sharply dressed, blonde woman is striding toward me with a grin on her face. It instantly puts my fears at ease. I don't see a knife or gun, so we're already off to a fantastic start from my daydreams.

When she gets within a couple of feet, her arms reach out wide for me. My body seems to be frozen in place because when her arms envelop me, mine are firmly at my sides. It doesn't deter her, though. A pleasant cloud of vanilla surrounds me in a secondary hug, and I feel my muscles begin to relax.

"Dani. I am so happy to meet you in person. You are gorgeous. Let me get a good look at you." Charlotte gushes as she leans back and holds onto my biceps while she inspects the rest of me. It feels weird. It feels dangerous. I know what lies beneath the heavy concealer and baggy sweatshirt. But I still try like hell to paste a smile on my face and hide the wince when she grips the bruises.

Charlotte's head tilts to the side. *Oh no.* Her eyes narrow as she steps closer and tilts my chin toward the sun. Her lips roll together tightly, and I swear an explosion of fire happens in her dark brown eyes. "Husband?"

Shit.

What am I supposed to say? No one has ever come out and asked. The practiced lies sit heavily at the back of my throat, unwilling to come out. Can I really tell someone what's happening to me? Maybe she could get my kids somewhere safe. I don't really care what happens to me. I'm dead one way or another. If my girls are taken care of, then my life's mission is fulfilled.

"Oh, Dani." Charlotte breathes out before wrapping me in her arms. I didn't realize my body was trembling until it felt like she was the only thing keeping me upright. It's the most comforting show of affection I've had in years. No wonder she's a therapist.

She leads me over to a little grassy knoll and gestures for us to take a seat. The fact that she seems not to think twice about putting her pristine white slacks against the dewy grass makes me even more comfortable with her. I'm used to entitled, prissy socialite types. Charlotte seems nothing like them. So when she asks me to tell her my story, I do.

* * *

This woman is like a whirlwind of protective, vigilante justice. I chose to trust this stranger blindly, but for some reason, it was the easiest decision I've ever made.

After I told her all the gory details of my relationship with Greg, she immediately jumped into action.

Step one: Get the essentials for the girls and me.

Step two: Charlotte checks us into a hotel in a neighboring city under her name.

Step two and a half: I sleep (mostly) soundly for the first time in decades.

Step three: Charlotte makes some mysterious phone calls to someone named "Jacobs" and asks for a favor.

Step four: All marital assets are transferred into my name only.

Step five: Greg's mugshot is plastered all over every local news channel. His previously strikingly handsome features are mottled with black and blue.

Step six: Sell everything.

Step seven: Board a flight to Alaska.

Step eight: Take a breath of fresh air while feeling safe.

Step nine: Leave the girls in the care of a woman named Emily, who Charlotte has sworn will take the best care of them.

Step ten: Face my past.

My damaged body shakes with nerves and excitement as we pull up to Charlotte's home. I can't believe this is where I am. Never in a million years did I think I would ever escape Greg, gain a new friend, and see my oldest friend and first love.

Laughter surrounds the homey space as Charlotte leads us into the kitchen. She continues on while I stand frozen in the entrance of the room. Time seems to stop as I stare at the back of the man before me. I note the subtle differences. But I would recognize him from any angle. Zachariah Thaddeus Morris.

I take a deep breath in and tap him on the back. Hours seem to pass as I wait for him to turn around.

A wide smile breaks out on my face as his emerald eyes widen comically. Shock, disbelief, and joy all filter over his face in mere seconds. His eyes dart to Charlotte and back to me.

"Hey there, stranger."

Chapter 15

Zach

Speechless. I am fucking speechless. *What? How?*

My eyes dart back and forth between Charlie and Dani. Once I finally decide that this is actually happening, I set my water on the counter and wrap Dani in my arms.

Her tiny body slots into mine, and I feel a peace wash over me that I haven't felt in a long, long time. Instead of thinking about the last time we saw each other and how my heart was ripped out, the happiness of our past envelops us. Coating our joined forms in a cloud of history, love, and laughter.

My eyes close as I rest my cheek on the top of her head. Her arms tighten as much as they can over my thick back. I don't know how long we stay wrapped in each other, but by the time we pull back, we are alone in the kitchen.

Before I can put too much thought into it, my hands cup her cheeks as I tilt her face up. "Dani. Lord, you are a sight for sore eyes. What are you doing here?" I ask in wonder. So many things are running through my mind. How is she here? Why is she here? How is she with Charlie?

A small chuckle leaves her, and a tear makes its way down her flushed cheek. I swipe it away with my thumb, and she places her hands on top of mine. "Seems we've got some catching up to do, cowboy."

* * *

Charlie must've known that I would be completely absorbed with Dani the moment she stepped foot in the house because the crowd quickly dispersed without so much as a word. Dani and I migrated to the living room; Charlie and Jason were also nowhere to be found.

It feels like I've stepped into a different time. A different world. One where tragedy and trauma hadn't taken place. Where we are just two 16-year-olds with nothing but bright futures ahead of us. Sparkles in our eyes, and fearlessness in our hearts.

But as it usually does, reality came slamming through the walls like the fucking Koolaid Man. It was unavoidable.

I could see the hesitancy in her eyes, so I went first. I don't know how long I poured my heart out to the first girl who ever held it, but to her credit, nothing but understanding flashed across her features. I left no stone unturned. No skeletons buried. She got it all. The good, the bad and the fucking nasty.

Honestly, the hardest part to tell her was the ins and outs of my relationship with Charlie. I'm not sure how much, if any, discomfort a first love has for a second love, but I wanted all my cards on the metaphorical table.

Above all else, Dani was my first best friend. Morgan and I have drifted over the years; she was my ex-wife's friend first, so naturally, the chasm grew between us after the messy divorce. I was too deep in my addiction to really give a fuck. *Shit. I owe Morgs an amends as well. Add it to the fucking list.*

So, of course, there was no animosity coming from Dani when

she heard about Little Bit and my history.

"Everything happens for a reason, Zee. I have to believe that. Otherwise, this whole existence is meaningless. All the pain and heartache was for nothing. We've learned lessons the hard way. But the thing about the hard way is it tends to sink into your bones. Forever etching itself into your very being so you don't make the same mistake again. Take Charlotte, for example—" Dani glances at a collage of photos next to the fireplace. Wedding photos. Date nights. Travels. A true montage of love and belonging. "Had she not experienced the hardships throughout her life, she wouldn't be as appreciative as to where it brought her. Those moments that make us hold on to the good things a little tighter because we don't know how long they will last. Your moment is coming, Zee. All of these bumps in the road have molded you into a better man than you could have imagined."

Words gather in my throat and get stuck. Emotions slam into me from all directions. It's not that I haven't heard these words before in one way or another, but for some reason, coming from her, it just hits differently. I link our fingers together and place a soft kiss on the top of her hand. "Thank you. Now, enough about me. Tell me about you."

Her hands tremble, and the soft smile on her face becomes harder and harder for her to keep up. I can see the moment that the weight of her past presses down on her shoulders. Clearly, things haven't been sunshine and roses for her either.

I don't rush her. I want to give her the same safe space that she's given me to empty my cup. I want my face to convey the patience and understanding that I feel for her. Bringing my other hand on top of our linked ones, I rub over the soft skin there. A move that I hope is comforting and not sleazy.

Dani inhales a shaky breath, and when her eyes lift from our hands to meet mine, they are filled with unshed tears. "Take your time. I'm here when you're ready, sweetheart." The endearment rolls off my tongue with ease. She closes her eyes, and the tears carve a path down her cheeks. I barely hear the whisper of her truth as she begins.

Chapter 16

Dani

It's so much easier to tell a stranger the darkness of your past than someone who has meaning in your life. When I poured my secrets out to Charlotte, it was more robotic and with very little emotion—like I was narrating a story of someone else's nightmare, not mine.

The trust I always had in Zach when we were kids has never wavered. Even though his colorful journey should dictate otherwise, I know his heart. I believe, with my whole being, that he is still that same boy, even if he doesn't see it.

I've disassociated from the hell I endured for all those years with Greg; I have to; otherwise, I'll fall down a deep, dark pit and never come out again. Explaining the abuse to Zach brings me right to the precipice of the pit. I see the flash of anger in his eyes. The clenching of his jaw. The rapid pulse beat in his neck. He wants to kill Greg. I get it; I do, too. But whatever strings Charlotte pulled, she assured me he will be in prison for a long, long time.

I've left out a key detail, though. My girls. I carry so much guilt and shame for keeping them around that environment for so long. I tried to be both parents and give double the love so they wouldn't feel so rejected by their father. The disappointed looks on their faces when he blew off a soccer game or recital. The shock on the parents' faces at the daddy/daughter dance when I dressed in a tux and whirled my girls around the dance floor. I would do anything for them. I would keep them safe at all costs, even at the disservice to myself.

Zach's breathing starts to come out in a pattern as we stare at each other, and I begin to count. He breathes in for one... two...three...four. And then out for one...two...three...four...five... six...seven...eight. Over and over, while never dropping his gaze from mine. I rub my damp palms along my jeans before reaching out for his hand. He takes it immediately. "There's a big piece missing from my story—" I take a deep breath in and let it out slowly as I try to prepare for the judgment on his face when I tell him. "I have daughters. Girls. Twins. Felicity and Olivia. They're eight."

While his eyes widen slightly in surprise, the judgment I was afraid of is nowhere in sight. As a matter of fact, his lips tip up in a genuine smile. My heart nearly stops. I'm so used to Greg's indifference to our kids that seeing a man who means something to me have such a positive reaction is a little jarring.

"Can I see a picture?" he asks, the smile on his face seeping deep into his voice.

A weird huff of laughter escapes me at his question. "W-what?" He wants to see them? He cares? He doesn't think I'm a crappy mom for having children with that monster? I ask him all these things with my eyes but still slowly slide my phone out.

I pull up some of my most recent favorites. We attended a child-friendly Paint & Sip night— wine for me, juice for them. The teacher took a photo of the three of us with paint smears all over us— faces, hands, clothes. We are a messy bunch. The smiles that she captured are radiant. And for once, I didn't have a black eye to hide behind loads of concealer and foundation.

After showing Zach what had to have been thousands of photos of the three of us, our laughter comes to a natural close. Both of us have tears in our eyes but for different reasons. His are joyous. Mine are pain-filled. These beautiful memories are filled with loving moments with my children, and that makes me beyond happy. But they are also laced with reminders of my pain. I can see the hurt in my soul through the lens of the camera. Why did I stay? This is the question that keeps me up at night.

"So, fuckface is in prison. You don't have any contact with his family, but what about yours? Your dad? Mom?"

I knew it would come up sooner or later. It's a difficult topic for me. I have no relationship to speak of with my mother. She ripped my dad's heart out with her affair with Zach's dad. She wasn't just cheating. She was in love with the man. My dad was never the same after we left my mom behind for Tennessee.

I was so angry at her that I refused to speak to her. I was sixteen, and she knew she couldn't force me to live with her, so when my dad asked for full custody, she gave it. Maybe we could have sorted through some of the pain and betrayal had she shown an ounce of remorse, but she didn't, at all. She wrote me a letter once, her last attempt at reaching out to me when I was eighteen. Honestly, I skimmed it. But one part put the proverbial nail in the coffin of our relationship:

"You can't help who you love. Your dad should've known that I wasn't happy. You'll understand when you're older."

The hell I will. I would never and will never be like her. My dad died without ever experiencing love and happiness again. He suddenly died of heart disease in my junior year of college. He was only forty-one. I was devastated. My mother didn't even bother to show up for the funeral.

All the damage she did to our family, and Mr. Morris didn't even want her at the end of it. He stayed with Zach's mom. Can't say I'm upset about that. You reap what you sow and all.

I don't want to dampen our reunion even more, so I give Zach a brief overview of what happened with my parents.

Yes, I'm alone. No, I don't want to go back to Tennessee. Yes, I'm terrified of what's next. No, I have no clue where we are going to live.

Charlotte set us up with a room at Ellie's House for now, but I don't see that working out in the long term. I haven't worked a job outside of being a stay-at-home mom in... ever, so my skills are limited for the workforce.

Shit. What do I do?

Chapter 17

Zach

After my housewarming party and the surprise of a lifetime, I drove Dani back to Ellie's House.

When we walk inside, fits of laughter come from the common room. Em is sitting on the floor with a video game controller in her hand next to who I assume to be Felicity and Olivia. Em's face is beet red, and it seems to fuel the laughter of the twins. I'm guessing whichever twin she's playing against is kicking her ass.

Dani creeps up behind the girls and spooks the hell out of them when she puts her hand on each of their shoulders. A chorus of "Mama!" filters through the open space. Leaning against the door frame, I just take it all in. It suits her, being a mom. She's always had such a big heart. Big enough for two.

"Oh no you don't!" One of the twins shouts and scrambles for the controller. Em has taken advantage of their temporary distraction to pull ahead in the racing game. "You can't cheat, Em! That's not fair! Felicity, tell her she can't do that." Olivia whines as she begins mashing buttons.

A triumphant Em stands and tosses the controller to the couch behind them. "And that, dear children, is how it's done." She bows like she just put on the show of a lifetime and received a standing ovation. When in reality, she is moments away from a shin kick from the two youngin's she just dishonorably bested.

Dani jumps in to save Em's tibia. "Girls, come over here. I have someone I want you to meet. He is a really old friend of mine." She wraps her arms around each of their shoulders. Two mini brunette versions of Dani stand before me, eyeing me warily.

I crouch down to their level and give them a wide smile. "Pleasure to meet you, ladies. My name is Zach. Now, who is who?"

The twin on the right curls her lip up and eyes her mom with irritation. "You're right, Mama, he *is* really old." The twin on the left smiles a bit but looks at me with apology instead of contempt.

Dani cackles out a laugh at my expense while I try to remind myself that this is an eight-year-old and I'm still in my prime at thirty-six. *Right? Right.*

She looks down at her daughter, laughter still filling her words. "Felicity, that's not a nice thing to say. I didn't mean he was old in age; I meant we have known each other since we were kids. Even younger than you two."

Okay, so Felicity hates me. I'm going to have to do something about that. But I know nothing about kids. And even less about girl kids. Maybe Dani can give me some tips later on.

* * *

Step one in my plan to win over the twins: feed them their favorite cuisine, followed by their favorite desserts.

The wrinkle in my plan is that, for identical twins, these girls are polar opposites. One loves seafood, the other hates it. One loves burgers, one is a vegetarian. Though Dani assured me that Felicity's vegetarianism is just a phase, and just last week, she chowed down on a whole package of bacon. So I decided that instead of going to a restaurant that will leave someone disappointed, I would take them all to my lake house for a picnic.

A very large order from YouBuyIFly later, and the four of us make ourselves a nice little spread on top of the blanket I laid out. Everyone got to order from wherever they wanted, and YouBuyIFly delivered it right to my door.

Dani and I both got steak sandwiches from Pizza Guy. Olivia got pad thai from Leaf of Lime. And Little Miss Vegetarian got veggie pizza and added bacon. I went to poke fun at her about it, and Dani almost stabbed me in the leg with her fork. She slyly shook her head while Olivia bit down on her lip to keep from giggling. Okay, so apparently here everyone knows bacon is now considered a "vegetable".

It was a good day. I've felt more happy and at peace with the three of them than I have in a very long time. We all just seem to fit together. I find myself wanting to know the kids more and wanting to get to know who Dani is now. Decades have separated us, and it's time to mend the gap.

A little part of me was really disappointed to drop them back off at Ellie's House... Okay, a big part of me. I really didn't want to fucking do it. But my house is still a disaster zone. The good thing that has come out of my hesitancy to be away from them is it's lit a fire under my ass to get the renovation moving.

As I walk into my "haunted lake house", *fucking Charlie*, I immediately begin to formulate a plan. I've got some vacation days saved up, and I think it's time I take them. They say you can't turn a hoe into a housewife. I'm about to prove that, yes, in fact, you can. With a little elbow grease, time, and a whole lot of money, I'll get this place in peak habitability. As quickly as humanly possible.

I've always been impulsive and have a habit of rushing into things without fully thinking them through. But this feels different. This feels right. I want to give these ladies the best that I can. I want them to have a safe space to live and the freedom to move around the house and be themselves.

Will Dani think I'm nuts when I ask her to move in? Perhaps.

Will it stop me from blazing ahead with my insane plan? Not in the slightest.

Chapter 18

Dani

It's taken two weeks. Two weeks to take a truly deep breath. To not worry about every little noise in the house, well, sometimes anyway. Even with a massive weight lifted off of my shoulders, I feel more exhausted than ever. A bone-deep depletion.

As hard as it was to leave the man I thought I would be with forever, I knew it was the right decision. He was never going to change, and even if he could, the damage had already been done.

My heart almost shattered yesterday when Olivia said she didn't realize I had such a big smile. As much as I tried to give them 100% of me, I was broken into too many pieces to succeed fully, it seems. And that kills me.

My children are happy. I am working on it.

I never realized how isolated Greg kept me. If it wasn't "his people," they weren't to be around. So, being seamlessly brought into Zach's friend group is as comforting as it is startling.

"Please let me help. I feel awful that you are always doing the cooking." I plead with Sally for what feels like the thousandth time this week. She has such a sweet spirit, and she's told me time and time again that feeding people is her love language. She feeds people; they feed her soul.

A crash startles us both, and our eyes dart to the living room where the twins are coloring. Shouting begins immediately, and I don't think or even take a breath before I'm running to the room for my children.

"Where is that cunt?" A very drunk, very dirty, and angry man slurs at me. I can feel the girls trembling behind me, and I make pointed eye contact with Sally. Hoping like hell she understands what I'm trying to say without words. *Take the girls and get help.* Thankfully, she does just that. And then there were two.

I'm no stranger to booze-drenched anger being shot in my direction. My hands go up in surrender to confirm I am not a threat. I steel my spine to keep myself rooted to the spot I'm standing. My fight-or-flight is going into overdrive, and everything in me says, *"Throw the lamp at his face and run."* But I don't. I can't. I don't know where Sally took the girls, and I'll be damned if I let this touch them. I didn't get us away from one vile situation to put us in another.

"I said, where is that fucking cunt?" he seethes and stalks closer to me. On instinct, I back up in slow steps. His rancid breath fans over my face as he brings us almost nose to nose. I open my mouth to respond, and the words fall away as he wraps a thick hand around my throat and squeezes.

"P-please. Stop. W-who are you looking for?" I plead through gasps of air. His hold becomes tighter as he lifts me up by the throat and slams me against the wall behind me. If I had any excess air, it would've just been ripped out of me with the force.

"Ruby!" *Ruby? The quiet new girl?* He spits in my face, and for the first time, his wild eyes focus as he takes in my form. A deep shudder flows through me as he brings his free hand up and squeezes my breast painfully. Black spots begin to cloud over my vision. *No. No! I will not be in this position again.* With what little energy I can muster, I lift my leg and smash it into his crotch as hard as I can. He hits the floor on his knees, dropping me on the way down.

Immediately, I feel temporary relief as oxygen floods back into my body and the dark spots begin to fade. The man recovers faster than I was prepared for, and I try to stand, but he grabs my ankle, and my weight collapses on my left elbow and wrist. A loud crack fills the room, or maybe it's just in my head.

Pain works its way up my arm. The man drags me back to him and flips me over. His pupils are blown wide, and darkness emanates from his entire body. Nausea wracks my stomach as he pins both wrists above my head with one hand. I barely have time to register the pain in my limbs when the back of his free hand connects with my cheek.

The black spots start to creep in again. A shrill ringing in my ear keeps me disoriented enough that I can't quite focus on one thing or another.

My pants are being ripped down my thighs.

My body freezes in place. Invisible chains lock me to the floor.

My underwear is ripped straight down the middle, and the sharp pain of the fabric stings against my hips.

No. Stop. Don't. Please don't do this.

I try to force the words from my lips as I feel him shimmy his pants down enough to free his hard length. Vomit crawls up my throat as he rubs the head of it across my C-section scar.

My mind wanders to a place. A place I know well. A grassy meadow with lightning bugs illuminating the air. A cool breeze flows through my hair, and a smile turns up on my lips as I lie down in between my girls, and we look up at the stars.

We count the ones that twinkle until we forget where we started and laugh. Their laughter fuels my soul. They are the best thing I ever did with my life. They make everything I've endured up to now worth it.

That's the last thought I have when the heavens break apart and fall down on me.

Chapter 19

Zach

Locking up my work truck, I remove my safety vest and head to my vehicle. It's been a long day. I just want to go home, take a shower and pass the fuck out.

Damn it. The flooring is almost done in the two guest rooms. I had hoped to be further along in the reno by now. But it seems the universe wants to fuck me six ways from Sunday.

If it's not a contractor issue, it's an availability issue. If I want gloss, they only have matte. I want this flooring, they only have that flooring. And on and on.

Once upon a time, I could've just hired a crew to do it all for me. Back when I was an entitled, rich prick with nothing better to spend my family's money on anyway. I don't think I'd use it even if I had it. I *want* to do the work. I want this to be *my* home. Something I've carved out just for me. And, hopefully, three beautiful girls that have turned my world upside down.

When I pull up to my house, the sunset over the water steals my breath. When was the last time I just sat and watched a sunset without overthinking everything? Deciding it's going to be right fucking now, I leave everything in the truck and climb on the hood. I stretch my body back, leaning against the windshield as I take in the watercolor show before me.

The sun sits low on the horizon, filling the sky with brilliant oranges, delicate pinks, and a splash of purple soaring through-out the expanse. The lake's water is so still that the magnificent display above me is perfectly reflected below.

I let my mind empty of everything. This moment here, with the light show and peace, is all I want to focus on.

When the sun finally dips down low enough that the colors fade, I jump off the hood. "Ah, fuck!" Instantly, I regret doing it when my feet hit the ground. I'm no spring chicken; my thirty-something knees can't take the beating that my twenty-something knees could.

It takes a few seconds to recover before I can get in the cab to grab my stuff. My phone vibrates against the cup holder. I fling my vest over my shoulder, grab my coffee cup, and stick it in my lunch box before tossing the strap on my other shoulder. Buzzing continues. Jesus, can't I get five seconds to get my shit inside.

The buzzing stops, and I finally get all my shit inside, toe off my boots, and set everything on the kitchen counter. This was the first room I completed. The kitchen is the second most important room in the house. Proceeded by the master bathroom, which is also completed.

Speaking of the bathroom, I need to drain the beast. Okay, that was douchey, even in my head.

My phone buzzes again as I re-enter the kitchen. I flip it over to find I have over thirty missed calls. What the hell? I have only one text, and it's from Charlie.

Call me NOW.

I don't hesitate for a moment. She wouldn't be this persistent if something wasn't wrong. The ringing of the line seems to go on for fucking ever. A rock sinks in my stomach as a barrage of scenarios floods my brain.

Charlie's voicemail picks up, and I damn near throw my phone at the wall. I hang up without a message and dial her right back. It takes four calls before she finally picks up. I am thoroughly frantic.

"Where the fuck have you been?" she barks at me. I wince a little at her tone. I haven't been on this side of Charlie's attitude in a long, long time. To be honest, I don't love it.

"I'm sorry, I just—" *Just what, was watching the sunset like a baby bitch? Lord.* I sigh. "I'm just getting home from work. What's going on, LB?"

Her words stop my heart cold. "Zach, Dani was attacked." The period hasn't even dried on her sentence before I've got my keys in hand and fly out the door to my truck.

* * *

"Zachy!" It took a long time for my body not to recoil when someone called me that. For many years, it just reminded me of Bex, and then I'm reminded of when everything in my life blew up. But that nickname coming from the four-foot shortcake with the tears in her eyes can call me whatever she wants. I don't know when these girls worked their way into my heart, but they are. And they are in deep.

I scoop Felicity up in my arms, and she immediately buries her face into my shoulder. "It's gonna be alright, darlin'. Let's go check on your mama and Livy." It's hard to remember a time when she was so distant from me. Though it's been mere weeks, the four of us have moved as somewhat of a unit. I don't know what the future holds, but at this point, I can't imagine letting any of them go.

Walking into the hospital room feels surreal, but I know I need to be strong for them. But when I lock eyes with Dani, I see the fear hiding behind her plastic smile. I know the smile is for the girls. She's so used to having to be strong 100% of the time. Livy jumps up, and I lift her with my free arm and sit the three of us in the chair beside Dani's bed.

Thank you, Dani mouths to me. Tears fall slowly, and I give her an understanding nod. I keep the girls cuddled up to me, giving them the comfort they need while giving their mother the freedom of feeling for a moment. Our silence is broken by the doctor entering the room with his nurse on his heels. He eyes me warily before asking if she wants me to step out; thankfully she declines.

The doctor goes over her injuries, which are mostly superficial. She'll be sore for a few days, but nothing is broken... except maybe her spirit. Nothing a little rest and ibuprofen can't fix, according to him. I think more like a little rest, ibuprofen, and running the fucker over with my rig. Like she can tell I'm starting to spiral a bit, Dani pats my hand while never breaking eye contact with the doc.

"I've got your discharge instructions here and have prescribed a higher-dose NSAID if you'd like it. Take it easy for a few days. The bruising will get worse before it gets better. If you have any concerns, please don't hesitate to call our nurse line."

His nurse hands the paperwork to Dani, and the doctor excuses himself to leave the room. The nurse lowers her voice, but the room is quiet enough that I still hear every word. "There's a matter of your bill, Mrs. Roberts. It seems that you are no longer on the insurance you provided. Do you perhaps have a new card or provider?"

Tears gather in her eyes. No, she doesn't. I gently move the girls off of my lap and grab my phone, pretending I'm getting a call.

"I've gotta take this. I'll be just outside the door. Holler if you need me." I press a soft kiss to the top of Dani's head and step into the hallway. I make sure to walk far enough away that my conversation won't be heard in her room.

As the ringing begins, my heart pounds. I'm doing this for Dani. But also... for myself. It's time.

Chapter 20

Zach

"Zachariah." His deep southern drawl is just as potent as ever. He may be in his eighties now, but he's still a force to be reckoned with. I can tell that with just one word.

"Papaw, I need you. I know I have no right to call you and ask for a favor, especially with how we left things before. I can't get fully into it right now, but I am sober, I went to rehab, and I'm really turning my life around. With that said, I'm really in a bind and need some money. I wouldn't ask if it wasn't important."

I feel my dignity and pride deflating like a balloon. I didn't want to need his money ever again. I wanted to carve my own path and prove that I could make it on my own. But this isn't a time to die on the hill of my ego. This is for Dani.

A frustrated sigh flows through the line, and I'm sure he's about to tell me to go fuck myself.

"It's about time, son."

"W-what?" I gasp out.

"I've been expecting your call. I'm glad you finally pulled your head out of your ass and reached out."

I don't even know what to say. The last time we spoke, I was arrested, and he told me too bad, get fucked. Okay, not in those words, but that was the gist of it.

He chuckles, and I stay confused as hell. "Did you forget who you listed on your forms as your emergency contact and HIPAA approval? I've been informed of your progress the entire time. That Charlotte is a delightful woman."

Little Bit? She's been in contact with my grandpa? Jesus. Maybe I should be concerned that she's nosed this much into my personal life. But all I feel is grateful. She still knows what I need before I do. Don't get me wrong, I'm still gonna give her a load of shit about it before I thank her.

I explain the situation with Dani and the hospital bill. "Consider it handled. Also, your trust is available to you. It has been since after the first phone call I got when you were in rehab. There's just one thing I want in return."

My thoughts are splattering about my brain like a bowl full of brownie batter and a mixer on full speed. He's taking care of the bill? He's restored my access to my trust? He takes my silence as permission to continue with whatever his demand may be.

"You call once a week and speak to your mee-maw. Her mind isn't what it used to be, but she still talks about you all the time. Sound fair?"

The air whooshes from my lungs. Fair? Millions of dollars for a weekly phone call? No, doesn't seem to be even at all. Doable? Absolutely.

"Yes, sir." Seems my words have all dispersed with the splatters of brownie batter.

"Good. And Zachariah? I expect you to come out to the Georgia estate soon."

* * *

Once I get Dani and the girls settled in the best hotel in River View—much to her stubborn refusal, which clearly didn't work with me— I head straight to see the little nosey vixen herself.

"You." I point at her as I enter her office. Thankfully, there were no patients. I really should've thought of that before barging in. But the smirk on her face tells me she probably got a phone call from Papaw and was waiting for this duel.

We face off silently for a moment. Our hands hovering over our metaphorical guns at our hips. A tumbleweed rolls across the space between us, and we draw. She gets off the first shot.

"Don't *you* me. I did what I did because I'm your friend, I love you, and I want you to have the support you deserve. You've come such a long way from the boy who steered your life down a dangerous path. You think you don't deserve good things, but you do, Zach. Hearing the way your papaw speaks about you and seeing the adoration in the eyes of Dani and her daughters tells me I did the right thing. So you can be upset with me for crossing boundaries if you want to, but if I had to do it over again, I wouldn't change a thing."

Well... fuck. Two shots straight to the head. This round belongs to her. Because what can I even say to that? She did what I would've always been too chicken shit to do. Both with Dani and Papaw. I can't even pretend to be mad about it. I'm elated. If you had asked me ten years ago if I ever thought this would be my life, I would've laughed in your face with a mouth full of whiskey.

"Naughty girl, LB. Come here." My features harden as I point to the floor in front of me. Not bothered at all, Charlie rolls her eyes and comes to stand before me. Her hands find her hips, and she glares up at me defiantly.

My eyes narrow at her, and I reach down, lifting her chin even higher with my index finger. "Thank you."

She tries to tamp it down, but a brilliant smile covers her mouth, and I can't help but return it. She wraps her arms around my middle, and we embrace in a soul-awakening hug. I always thought Charlie and I were destined to be together— soul mates. And we are, but just not in the way I had thought. I'm grateful to have her in my life, and this is the way it should be.

A stray thought occurs to me. "LB, why didn't you try to reach out to my sperm donor?"

She pulls back and quirks an eyebrow at me like the answer should be obvious. I know what she'll say before she does, and she's right. I'm glad she didn't try to mend that dead-end. "Some broken things should stay broken."

My parents are a sore subject. They moved back to Georgia. I talk to Mama every now and again, but I haven't spoken to the coward who sired me in years. And I don't see that changing any time soon, if ever.

"Speaking of broken things, my trust has been restored, and with what happened at Ellie's House, I want my renovation completed ASAP. I don't blame anyone for what happened, but EH is not a place for a woman and her children. Do you have some recommendations for a contracting company?"

Chapter 21

Dani

Spending three weeks in a luxury hotel was really no skin off my nose, but when Zach asked the girls and me if we would move in, the answer was an immediate yes. I use the term "asked" loosely. He told us we would be moving in. And honestly, no part of me even wanted to decline.

The property is beautiful. The house backs up to a serene private lake with splendid mountain views. Dang, I sound like an ad for a real estate company. But it's true. Alaska is breathtaking. Not that I need my breath taken any more than it has been lately. But this is at least a refreshing way to do so.

We each got our own rooms. Liv and Lissy were so pleased with that. As twins, they tend to share everything, but they are such different people that I think having their own space to be unique is just what they need.

We've fallen into an easy routine. I tend to the house and garden that Zach had put in for me. The girls started at the local prep school at Zach's insistence. And the man himself puts in an honest day's work, day after day. He hasn't asked for anything in return for all of his generosity. I've always known the man had a heart of gold, but I never expected this kind of treatment in my life.

We've been avoiding having talks about where the two of us stand, relationship-wise. Are we friends? Are we more? Do we want to be? These are all extremely difficult questions for many reasons. I don't think either of us is in a place to be in a romantic relationship, though I wouldn't fault him if he wanted to find someone to fill that void. It just can't be me.

I love Zach with everything I have. It's always been that way. But I'm not that girl anymore... now I'm broken. Greg broke me, and my body has betrayed me. Zach deserves more than I could ever give him, emotionally and physically. But I can't keep putting off the conversation. We need to discuss what happens next.

* * *

After the most delicious steak I've had in my life, I decided tonight was the night. The girls have gone to their rooms for the evening, and Zach has the day off tomorrow. We can't put it off any longer.

We clean the kitchen side-by-side; it's so easy with him. I have my best friend back again, and all feels right in my world—almost. I pour each of us a glass of sun tea, and we take up what has become our nightly ritual of sitting in the Adirondack chairs on the back porch. Watching the sun as it sets over the mountain and soaking up the peace in the air.

When the last of the light fades behind the mountain, I speak up. "What are we doing here, Zach?"

He stays silent for too many heartbeats while he sips his tea. My pulse drums rapidly under my skin. It feels like, at any moment, it's going to burst out and do a jig on the deck.

"I've been thinking about that. I love you. You know that. And I love the hell outta those girls of yours. But I also know that neither of us is in a place where we can add more complications to our lives. So, let's just be us. Is that okay?"

The utter relief that flows through my body is so unexpected. I don't know why I didn't give him more credit. I thought maybe he'd be upset or push for more. But he said it exactly the way I feel about it.

"That's very okay. Thank you so much for everything. I can't explain how much you've changed our lives. I never thought this was possible." I'm trying so hard to hold back my tears, but my voice cracks, giving away the emotional tidal wave that is threatening to take me under.

"Freedom?" he asks.

"Peace. Safety. Contentment."

It's true. I lived a constant nightmare for years. I was sure I would die at Greg's hands, and it would just be swept under the rug by his family and connections. I feared more for the girls' future than my own. They've always been my top priority, and it will always be that way. I would give them anything. Give *up* anything.

Zach has been more of a dad to them in the last couple of months than Greg has been their whole lives, and it shows in their reactions to him. He helps them with their homework, sings to them, dances with them, and builds pillow forts—all the things a parent should do to be close to their children, and they don't even share DNA.

We've made ourselves a life here. A home. A family. All because some crazy lady stalked me, flew out to talk to me, and flipped my world on its ass in the best way. I owe so much to Charlotte for pulling me out of that hell and giving me the tools

I needed to pick myself up off the floor and move forward.

I have all I want now. A beautiful, *safe* home. Happy children. A life partner who still has a fantastic ass but an even better heart. Friends that *I* chose. If I were to die tomorrow, the only thing I would regret is not having more time to live the life I deserve. Because I do, I know that now, I deserve this. *We* deserve this.

"Hmm. Do me a favor, would you?" Zach asks and reaches out a hand to me. When I put my hand in his, he gently pulls, letting me know he wants me to stand. I oblige and get hit with a sudden wave of dizziness. I wave off his concern when it passes and stand before him.

He stands and moves me back a little further, turning us so the lake is in our periphery. The wind flows gently through the trees and lands on the surface of the calm waters, causing a steady stream of ripples in its wake.

Closing my eyes, I soak up the serenity of the moment. When I open them again, I don't quite understand what I'm looking at.

"Uh, Zach? Why are you down on one knee?"

He gathers my hands in his. His emerald eyes sparkle as he smiles that crooked smile that I love so much. "Danica Jane Swenson—" I smile, and internally, I'm kicking my feet like a school girl that he calls me by my maiden name. "— you were my first everything. But above all, you were my first best friend. And that title is yours still. I love you and those rugrats so damn much. All I want is to take care of the three of you and continue living this life we're building. Part of that is making sure the three of you have everything you need, including insurance. So... Dani, sweetheart, sugarbee. Will you do me the honor of becoming my third and final wife?"

I burst out laughing, and when he doesn't join me, I realize he's serious. He wants us to get married? But... didn't we just say we were remaining friends? Did I hallucinate that entire conversation?

"Stop spinning out right now, darlin'. I want us to get legally hitched so that you all are protected. You don't have insurance, but I have a great plan with the city. Also, I couldn't think of a more deserving trio to be spoiled and looked after for the rest of our time on this earth. It doesn't have to mean anything beyond that. We don't even have to tell anybody if you don't want to."

"You're serious?" I ask, completely flabbergasted.

Zach winks at me and reaches into his back pocket before presenting me with a sparkling ring. "Serious as a heart attack. So, what'll it be, honey tits?"

"Honey tits?"

He waves off my indignation. "We'll work on the pet names."

Can I actually do this? There are so many reasons why it's not a great idea, but still, I want to say...

"Yes."

Chapter 22

Dani

We decided to have a small ceremony, non-traditional, of course. Nothing in our lives is traditional.

In Alaska, you don't have to have someone ordained to perform your wedding, so we asked Charlotte to marry us. It seemed only fitting since she was the one who had brought us back together after all. She read the words off of a script we grabbed from the courthouse. We decided to skip all the religious vows and opted to write our own. And when I say write, I mean we stood in a semicircle, holding hands with my daughters, and pledged our love and faithfulness to *them*.

Charlotte's husband's friend, Jacobs, managed to get Greg to sign away his rights. I don't want to know any details about the hows or whys. That doesn't matter now. All that matters is that we are all happy. I've never been a vengeful person, but if there's anyone I hope steps on a hornet's nest, it's him—he's allergic.

Our wedding rings are simple platinum bands with diamonds marking the Gemini constellation. On the inside, all four of our names are engraved. It's a ring that binds us together as a family. Our bond is etched in our hearts as deeply as it is in the precious metal.

With only a handful of what have become *our* friends, we became a legal family unit. Well, we will be soon. Tonight, Zach is going to ask the girls if he can adopt them and give us all a new last name. He's so cute and nervous about it, but those girls adore him, and he has nothing to be scared of.

I dreamed of this day for so long as a kid. Deep in my soul, I felt that one day, I would be his wife. We just took a wild route to get there. It means something a little different now than I had anticipated when I was a young girl with stars in her eyes and ignorance of the world in her heart.

It's been just me for so long. I may have had a husband, but I was a single parent. If it were anyone else on the planet, I would've told him he was nuts and run like hell in the other direction. But Zach is... Zach. He's always made me feel safe and secure. If there's anyone I trust to take care of *our* girls in my absence, it's him.

* * *

Exhaustion reigns supreme over every other feeling. It's been a long, eventful day. Now that everyone has left, the four of us sit on the back deck. The girls convinced Zach to line it with fairy lights. Though, it wasn't hard to convince him at all. Liv and Lissy have him wrapped around their identical fingers.

"Be right back," Zach says, giving me a conspiratorial wink as he skips, yes, skips, into the house. The girls are oblivious as usual, but he's about to make their night. He comes back out with a picnic basket and sets it in between their chairs. He stands both girls up in the very same spot he had me when he *proposed*.

Giggles fill the air, and my heart feels lighter than it has in a long time. Zach gives them a speech about how much he loves and cares for them. He hands each of them a flute of sparkling cider before dropping down on one knee and presenting them with matching rings to mine. They waste no time between squeals and launching themselves at him.

The three of them collapse in a chuckling heap. I close my eyes and take it all in. I hope to keep this memory fresh in my mind forever. I never want to lose this feeling. More than that, I hope Zach holds on to it forever. He's going to need to cherish the good times.

* * *

"Mrs. Morris, thank you so much for waiting. Please follow me," the nurse says with a smile. What is she happy about? This is not a happy moment—not for me, at least. I had a feeling. I've felt something was off for quite some time, but I was afraid—afraid to know the truth, afraid to think of what came next.

Everything I've done in the last few months has been in preparation for this possibility. I know that if the worst happens, the twins are taken care of. Now that Zach is back in my life, I know that they will take care of him, too.

Zach's insurance is fantastic, but I still don't want to spend a bunch of time and money trying to outrun fate. I should've come much, much sooner. I'm a ticking time bomb, and I'd rather just live life to the best of my ability until I can't.

I've struggled with my decision to deal with this alone. But I don't want people to mourn me while I'm still here. I can't stand the thought of frightening the girls. I know it's probably as selfish as it is selfless, but it's what I've chosen, and I'm determined to stick with my choice until the end.

I came into this world alone. I've felt alone for most of my life. It's only fitting I should leave it alone.

Chapter 23

Zach

Dani is starting to worry me. Lately, it seems she can barely get out of bed or walk up the stairs. Yesterday, I thought I was going to have to rush her to the emergency room. When she took the blanket off of her lap and stood from the couch, it looked like she was smuggling water balloons under the skin of her ankle. She waved me off and said it happens sometimes, and it's nothing to be concerned about. How the fuck is what used to be a dainty ankle turning into a gelatinous mass nothing to be concerned about?

Next week is our six-month wedding anniversary. Just because we aren't a romantic couple doesn't mean I can't spoil the shit out of her. She's still my forever person. Em is coming over to watch the kiddos, and I'm taking my girl out on the town. I hope like hell this raises her spirits. It doesn't seem like much does these days.

I rented a badass sports car to get us to the restaurant in style. Dani doesn't need high class; we are the same in that way. But she deserves to spend a night in luxury with people waiting on her hand and foot. So I asked Charlie's best friend, Savvy, to pick up a swanky dress and shoes in Dani's size. I didn't want her to have to think about anything. The night is all about freeing ourselves from the day-to-day. We leave the parent titles at the door and slide into us as people.

As much as it makes me sound like a pussy, I can't wait to connect more with Dani on a deep, spiritual level. I want to know all about adult Dani. What are her hopes and dreams? What does she see the future for the girls looking like? What about our future? What's her bucket list? Does she still want to travel? Does she still want to hit every Disney park worldwide? So many things to uncover about my oldest friend.

* * *

"Okay, what is so urgent that I had to come over straight after work, LB? I look and smell like ass."

She rolls her eyes and ushers me inside to the living room where Jason awaits, looking awkward instead of his usual serial killer face. "Y'all are making me nervous. Am I about to become an episode of *The First 48*?"

Charlie and Jason share a look, and my carefree feeling begins to deflate. "Uh, guys, I was fucking around. What's that look about?"

"Last week, I was talking to Dani, and she shared a conversation you had with her not too long ago."

"Okay…" Where is this going? We have conversations all the time. What did we talk about that could need a third party's interference?

"It's about Rebecca Crowe. Bex." Charlie doesn't break eye contact as mine shoot open as wide as saucers. I was not expecting this.

"What about that cun— erm, person?" I ask.

"I get the feeling you haven't kept up with her at all. You never brought it up, so neither did I, but now I think that was a mistake."

"I don't give a rat's ass what she's doing with her life. Why would we talk about it? Give it to me straight, LB. What's going on?"

Jason clears his throat, drawing my attention to him instead. "Long story short? She's dead."

Oh. Okay, I mean, I don't know what I'm supposed to feel about that. I fucking hate her. She ruined my life. I wished her dead many times over the years. I don't feel bad, but I guess I don't really feel anything. But I suppose the right thing to do as a human is to pretend to care since my friends deemed it important enough to have a special meeting about it. "Oh. What happened? Car accident?"

"Nah. Charlie killed her."

"Jason! For fuck's sake." Charlie shouts, and my eyes bounce between them, trying to make sense of the words flowing between us.

"Ow. Don't hit me. You did." Jason whines, and it sounds so unnatural that I can't help but chuckle at the sight.

"Yeah, but you don't just say it like that."

"Like what?"

"Like I'm a goddamn psycho who goes around killing people!" Charlie whisper shouts, even though it's only the three of us in the room.

I lift my hand like a kid in class. "Uh, excuse me. You fucking did what?"

Charlie lets out an exasperated sigh like I'm the one who's causing the ruckus in the conversation. For real, what the fuck is happening? "Okay, okay. Don't get your panties in a twist,

Zach. So like ten years ago, Rebecca used one of Priests' runners, Bennie, to hatch a revenge plan."

Priest was the drug lord who abused Charlie when she was a teen. He damn near killed her with a needle and that's what started her journey to hospitalization and recovery. He got what was coming for him at his trial when the sister of one of his other victims shot him point blank in the courthouse. She then turned the gun on herself, which I learned later was a trigger point for me and my degrading mental health.

Priest used the same group of guys to deal in his territory. Erick, Rick and Bennie. I'm not familiar with any of them besides Erick and he's on my shit list for how he treated Charlie back then too.

"Revenge? For what? You didn't do anything to her." I grit out between clenched teeth. Fucking Bex, good riddance bitch.

"In her mind, I did. I stole you. Even though, you know, we'd been together for two years, and she sexually assaulted you by drugging you and pretending she was me."

"Jesus. That bitch is on a whole different level of reality. Or I guess, *was*." I sigh and shake my head, trying not to go back to the memories from those days. They haunted me for many years, and I'm not keen to dip back into them.

"Yeah. Delusional doesn't even begin to cover it. She pulled Bennie into her plot, and he kidnapped me. Kept me drugged and restrained for days. He beat me and did other things..."

My heart drops at the words she doesn't say. "I'll kill him," I growl as a whirlwind of emotions slam into me all at once. I'm angry at Bex for entering either of our lives. I'm happy she's dead. I'm murderous. I'm devastated.

"Oh, don't worry. Jason did that. He swooped in and saved me at the last moment before both Rebecca and Bennie were about to cross that final line of assault and, ultimately, my murder."

Surprised, I eye Jason, and he simply shrugs like it's no big deal. But I suppose that just proves his devotion to his woman. He literally killed for her. Not many wives can say that. Probably for good reason, but in this case, totally warranted.

Charlie continues. "Jason went after Bennie. There was a struggle for the gun he pointed at Jason's head. But in the end, Jason got the best of him and got the shot off first. Rebecca was trying to finish what Priest couldn't and force me to OD. The shot distracted her enough that I was able to get the syringe from her and plunge it into her eye. She fell backward, clipped her head on the counter, and that was that. Our monsters vanquished in the blink of an eye..." She looks at both Jason and me with expectant eyes, which we return with confusion. "Come on, blink of an eye! Like, because she only had one at that point. You know what? Whatever. It's not funny if I have to explain it."

This woman. I jump up from my seat and lift her into my arms for a tight, long overdue hug. "Thank you. If you hadn't, I would've for what she did to you. I'm so sorry she came into our lives. I'm glad you made it through." She squeezes me back just as tightly. I meet Jason's gaze over her head, and we have a silent conversation in which I thank him for saving her.

"I've had a lot of time to work through that particular trauma, so I can make punny jokes every now and again. Don't get me wrong, the nightmares creep up sometimes, but it's not very often, and I know my dark knight is beside me to slay any demons that try to come for me."

I can't even be upset with Dani for telling her about our talk. I told her all about Bex, the bad, the worse, and the horrible. I also shared that I had a tiny bit of fear that she would pop back up unexpectedly. When I didn't have anyone to care for, it didn't matter. But now? Those three girls are my world, and I would never let any harm come to them. I wasn't kidding when I said I would've killed her.

"Thank you, Little Bit. Thank you."

Chapter 24

Zach

The night of our anniversary has finally arrived. It's been a rough week. I think Dani's coming down with something, but she assured me she'd love nothing more than to go out tonight. And I can't wait to show off my suit.

Since gaining access to my trust again, I haven't used it much. I wasn't fucking around when I said I wanted to make my own way. But I can't lie; it does come in handy to have that kind of money at my disposal.

As soon as the ink was dry on my marriage certificate, I legally adopted the twins, and all three of them took my last name. I opened two college funds with enough money to send them to any school of their choice. I also invested a bit, which will be my gift to my girls when they graduate college.

As much as I don't want them growing up entitled, I want them to have every opportunity to have an amazing life. Just like I want for their mama. And if I'm in the position to provide that, why shouldn't I?

After a chorus of "aw" and "Damn Dan's! I didn't know you had an ass like that!" That came from Em, of course. We got into the convertible I rented and made our way to the snazziest restaurant I could find.

I've got a plan. First, we dine like kings. Then we dessert like children loose in a candy store. Then, off to the museum for our own light show and personalized tour. Finally, to top the night off, stargazing at the top of Sky Ridge.

The restaurant is so fucking uppity. I've been around wealth many times in my life, but this is just over the top. I'm sure most of the patrons are in the 1%. Glitz and glamour shine everywhere you look.

"Well. We're here, so we might as well get our fancy grub. My lady?" I hold my arm out for her to hook hers through, and we make our way to the host stand. We're seated immediately because, of course, money talks. Especially in the service industry. I also know the staff have to put up with these yuppy fucks so I want to make it worth their while.

Dani turns down the wine selection even though I told her it was totally okay if she wanted a glass. She said her throat was a little sore, so she opted for some hot tea instead. We devoured the appetizers, which were way too fucking small. When the next course came out and was equally small, Dani and I had the same thought. "Fuck this. Let's go get burgers."

We're running close to getting to the museum, so we grab our burgers and eat them on the way. It kinda feels like I'm in that episode of *How I Met Your Mother* when Ted takes Stella on the two-minute date.

Dani stumbles a bit, and I catch her arm as she exits the car. She nearly drops her chocolate shake. "Brain freeze?" I tease with a chuckle. She seems a little unsteady but gives me a tight smile and nods. Okay, that's a little weird.

The tour was... well shit, the tour was boring. It just felt like something fancy people would do, I forgot to account for the fact that neither of us are particularly interested in art. But, the light show was totally rad. It was like being on LSD without ever taking a drop. You know those dancing lights on the computer music players in the 90s? Like that, but all around you. An immersive trip for the sober.

After we gathered our wits and were no longer disoriented from the impromptu rave, we headed for Sky Ridge. It's a warm night, so I let the top down. No longer worried about messing up Dani's gorgeous curls, which I'm sure took hours to do.

It's a perfect fucking night for stargazing. Not only is the sky crystal clear, but earlier today, when I checked the weather, there was an Aurora sighting alert. The chances that the Northern Lights will come out to play while we are here are almost 100%. Nature's light show is not one you want to miss, and it's extra special because it'll be Dani's first time seeing them in person. I get to pop her cherry, twice!

We let our seats back so we can get comfortable and watch the stars while waiting for the show to begin. I hand Dani her favorite throw blanket from the house, and she tucks it all around her body, leaving just her head exposed. I guess she's not used to the Alaskan weather yet. When I say it's a warm night, it's in the low 60s with a slight breeze.

I reach into the console and pull out two rolls of frosted chocolate donuts and two Yoohoo's. She takes them when I offer but sets the treats in her lap while I quickly dive into mine.

"You ever wonder what's next?" she asks, keeping her eyes on the celestial expanse.

"You mean in life or after life?"

"After. I don't really subscribe to the whole 'heaven and hell' thing. I think our souls drift through the universe, looking for the perfect star. The one that's shined on us our whole lives.

The one we've wished on more times than we can count. The one that got us through the darkest of nights. That's what I hope, anyway."

"Wow. That would be really fucking cool. I don't know. I always just assumed there was nothing. Just lights out, and that's it. But I like your version much better, so let's go with that. Though, we don't have to worry about that for a long time, sweetheart. We've got many more good years with our girls and each other." I lean over and plant a soft kiss on her clammy cheek. I really need to get her some cold medicine or something.

"Yeah. I like my version better, too."

"Who would've thought you and I would be here? Married. Talking about our futures and our kids. Shit, Dani. You three? You've saved my life. You've *made* my life. I'm so thankful for you. I love you."

"I lo—" A sudden coughing fit cuts off her words. I hand her a napkin, and we both look at it and each other when she pulls it away from her mouth.

Blood.

Chapter 25

Zee,

First, I want to thank you. You came back into my life exactly when I needed you the most, and I can't express to you how grateful I am. You've made the last year of my life amazing.

I loved watching your relationship with our daughters grow and flourish. I think that's what finally gave my body permission to stop fighting and accept the inevitable.

Witnessing them decide to call you Dad was one of the happiest moments of my life. I leave this world knowing that the three of you have each other. I trust you with their well-being, just as I trust that you won't hold anger and hurt in your heart forever from my omission.

I know I'm leaving a lot on your shoulders, and for that, I am sorry. I want you to know I have no regrets. I am happy to be your wife. You won't want to hear it now, but don't make me your last.

You deserve love, Zach. You've been so terrified of relapsing into old behaviors that you've completely overlooked the amazing man you've become. Up until we connected again, my dad was the only truly good man I've ever met. You've joined him at the top of that list.

Give yourself time to grieve my loss and then some more to find a new normal with the girls. When you feel that ache just a little less and the days get easier, that's when you'll know it's time. Time to open your heart once more.

I'm okay with another woman taking care of our kids if you believe them to be worthy of the title. I know they will always come first for you. But please, don't let them forget me. I've included a letter for each of them. I'm leaving it up to you to decide when it's the right time to give it to them. I fear they are too young to really understand it as intended right now.

Your heart is too beautiful to stay hidden and not shared with the world. Promise me you won't hide behind your pain and that you'll continue to live for yourself and our daughters.

Speaking of the girls, the teenage years are going to be rough. Remember, you're strong, and you got this. Two little girls can't get the best of you. But seriously, reach out to our friends; they will help you through the roughest of it.

You'll doubt yourself and feel like you're not doing it right. But I'll let you in on a little parenting secret: We all feel that way. We're all just trying our best not to damage our children to the point of intensive therapy. We are learning along the way, just as they are. You will do great. You are an amazing dad and an even better man.

I love you, Zachariah Thaddeus Morris. I did then, I do now, and I will for eternity.

Look for me in the stars, okay?

With all my love, Dani

Epilogue

Zach

I can't believe it's been nearly ten years since we lost Dani. I thought the massive heart attack was sudden and out of nowhere. I was shocked to learn that not only was she in late-stage heart disease, but she knew at least for a while and never told me.

I ignored what now seems like some pretty obvious signs. I took her at her word that it was nothing or it was just normal girl stuff. Like an idiot.

It took me a long time to forgive myself and to not be a little angry with her for not telling me and going through that pain alone. I tried to do what she asked in her letter. But sometimes, I'm just a stubborn son of a bitch.

I am going against one of her requests, though. She will be my last wife. I have no interest in getting married for a fourth time. Any casual relationships I've had over the years have had that clearly explained to them from the get-go. I wasn't interested in wasting anyone's time.

She was all too right about those teenage years. Boy, I went to bed one night with sweet angels and woke up to hell beasts crying over split ends. Charlie, Savvy, Em, and even Ari were all saving graces for me during the worst of it. They helped so much.

I had no clue what the difference was between a pad, a tampon and a fucking cup. Why are women's hygiene products so invasive? In this day and age, you would think there'd be a better solution by now.

I damn near fell out when Liv asked me to make her a birth control appointment. Thankfully, I kept face in front of her. But best believe when I went to Charlie's later that day, I flipped my fucking lid. She was having sex? At sixteen? I'm a fucking hypocrite, I was getting my dick wet even earlier than that. But, she's my little girl, damn it. It's different.

I was relieved when Felicity brought home her first girlfriend. She seemed so worried about my reaction. I hugged them both and told them that as long as they were happy, I was happy. I left out the part where I was internally doing cartwheels that at least one of my kids wasn't going to make me a grandpa before I was ready.

But still, because I'm the worry wart dad, I sent the twins an email with safe sex practices and pamphlets for whichever gender they prefer. I could not look them in the eye for days. It was important, though. At least to me, it was. They probably already knew the information, but I wanted to be doubly sure they were protected and had resources.

"Fuck me, why is it so hot on the one day we have to sit outside for hours?" Em whines beside me while she fans herself with the program.

"I told you not to wear a sweater. There wasn't a cloud in the sky this morning. It was bound to be hot and sunny for the ceremony." I reply, rolling my eyes at her. She never listens to me. Seven years that we've been together now, and all my words still go in one ear and out the other.

"Yeah, I don't think you said that."

"Oh, I most definitely did. Now hush. They're up next."

Some hoots and hollers come from the audience as my girls, my pride and joys, my reason for living, walk across the stage and accept their diplomas. A tear runs down the side of my face, and Em elbows me in the ribs. "Such a sap, big daddy."

"Shut up. I'm so damn proud of them. They've grown into such amazing women. Dani shines through their eyes and their hearts daily. And honestly, I'm just glad I didn't fuck that up. It was rocky there for a while."

Even though she was giving me shit, Em's shouts overtake everyone's when the girls walk down from the stage and take their seats. They grin from ear to ear at her. They've always loved Em, and when we decided to become a "thing", I was so worried to tell them. I shouldn't have been. They couldn't wait to start calling her Mama Em.

I honored Dani in our house, then and now. She was never forgotten. Her name was never whispered and always spoken with love and joy. Pictures of all of us dot several walls. Em has never batted an eye. There is no animosity, no drama. That's one of the things I love about her. Even though neither of us is interested in getting the government involved in our relationship, we do love each other.

I had to lose most of my loved ones. I hit a horrible rock bottom and nearly lost my life. I spent decades playing fast and loose with morality. But somehow, someway, something decided I was worthy of a second chance.

A chance to prove that I could be a better man. I've spent every day since making a conscious effort for that to be the case. As I look at the two beautiful girls in front of me and the irritating, amazing woman beside me, I know that I have. And I'll do whatever it takes to keep it that way.

"Daddy!" the twins shout at the same time, much to their dismay. They do that a lot. I gather them both in the tightest of daddy bear hugs, whispering my praises in their hair. Olivia grabs Em by the waist and brings her into our family hug because that's what we are: a family. It doesn't look the way I thought it would, but that makes it all the more special.

"So, what now?" Em asks as we make our way to the car.

In unison, the girls shout, "Graduation party!"

Oh fuck.

The End

Afterword

Life doesn't always turn out the way we expect. This story is a prime example. It may have been unconventional, but in the end, Zach got the love he needed and deserved. I wanted this journey to showcase that unconditional love, whether from a romantic partner, best friend, or two amazing little girls, is enough to give anyone a HEA.

Not everyone's road to recovery has a happy ending. My goal is to give hope that it is possible. This may be a fictional story, but the despair, anger, and uncertainty are very real.

Thank you so much for following Zach on his journey. It's been a heavy road so far in the River View universe, so get ready to laugh your ass off in Savvy's rom-com-esque, rivals-to-lovers story— Supernova — coming soon!

As always, this wouldn't have been possible without my amazing Alpha/Beta Team. Their feedback is valuable and important to me. Also, thank you to the ARC readers for giving their time and reviews!

I appreciate all readers who give my stories a chance. Please consider leaving a review.

Suicide Prevention Hotline or Call 988 for additional resources.

SAMHSA (Substance Abuse and Mental Health Services Administration) – Offers a national helpline (1-800-662-HELP) and treatment locators in the U.S.

The National Domestic Violence Hotline – 24/7 confidential support (Call: **800-799-7233** or Text: **START** to 88788)

If you are struggling with your mental health or addiction, you don't have to face your pain alone. Help is available, and there is a path forward, no matter how impossible things may seem right now. Your story is still being written, and there are brighter chapters ahead. Stay.

Join my Facebook reader group for all things River View and upcoming projects. Members get first dibs on ARCs. I post teasers and give exclusive looks at my WIPs and new covers! See you there!
   I See You Coralee-Reader Group

For signed paperbacks, visit my website
   www.cltaylorbooks.com/store

Follow me on socials for Bookish content
   Tiktok @coraleetaylorauthor
   Instagram @coraleetaylorauthor

More By Coralee Taylor

Ties That Bind Series

1. I See You, Charlotte
2. I Hear You, Charlotte
3. I Choose You, Charlotte

Fated Hearts of River View Series (Standalone's)

1. If I Were A Better Man-novella
2. Supernova
3. The Stars Over Norsville

www.ingramcontent.com/pod-product-compliance
Lightning Source LLC
Chambersburg PA
CBHW031057310726
48969CB00007B/2320